JT
The Making of a Total Legend

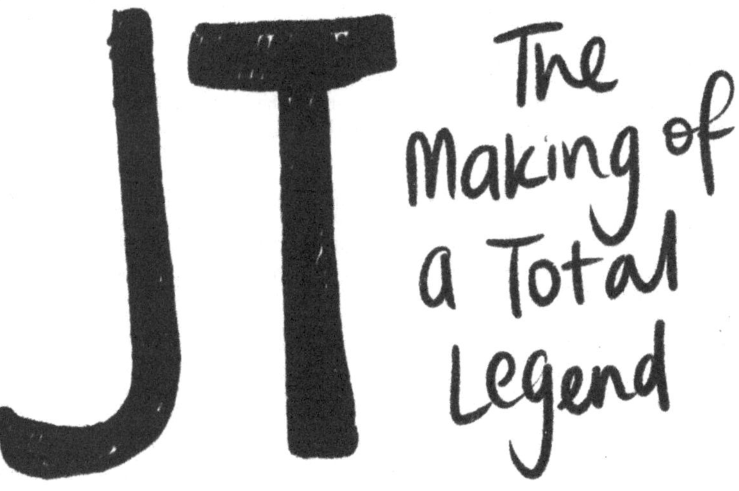

JOHNATHAN THURSTON

with JAMES PHELPS

HarperCollinsChildren'sBooks

HarperCollins*Children'sBooks*

First published in Australia in 2019
by HarperCollins*Children'sBooks*
a division of HarperCollins*Publishers* Australia Pty Limited
ABN 36 009 913 517
harpercollins.com.au

HarperCollins *Publishers*
Macken House,
39/40 Mayor Street Upper
Dublin 1, D01 C9W8, Ireland

HarperCollins*Publishers*
Level 13, 201 Elizabeth Street, Sydney NSW 2000, Australia
Unit D1, 63 Apollo Drive, Rosedale, Auckland 0632, New Zealand
A 53, Sector 57, Noida, UP, India
1 London Bridge Street, London SE1 9GF, United Kingdom
Bay Adelaide Centre, East Tower, 22 Adelaide Street West, 41st floor, Toronto, Ontario M5H 4E3, Canada
195 Broadway, New York NY 10007, USA

A catalogue record for this book is available
from the National Library of Australia

ISBN 978 1 4607 5861 8 (paperback)
ISBN 978 1 4607 1238 2 (ebook)

Cover design by Hazel Lam, HarperCollins Design Studio
Cover image © National Rugby League (15714955)
Typeset in Sabon LT Std by Kelli Lonergan
Printed and bound in Australia by McPherson's Printing Group
The papers used by HarperCollins in the manufacture of this book are a natural, recyclable product made from wood grown in sustainable plantation forests. The fibre source and manufacturing processes meet recognised international environmental standards, and carry certification.

For Frankie, Charlie, Lillie and Remie …

you are my inspiration.

CHAPTER ONE

IT WAS MOSTLY PINK, soft and fluffy on top, rock-hard and ribbed on the bottom. And boy, did it hurt.

'No, Mum,' I pleaded. 'Not the slipper. Please. I'm sorry.'

Too late ...

Mum had already turned her night-time footwear into a weapon. Kicked from her foot and caught in hand, the slipper was a whip: cocked and ready to crack.

'You are getting it, boy,' she howled. 'You can't behave like that.'

We got yelled at when we were bad. We got the slipper when we were worse.

'Come here now,' she said, her voice all no-nonsense and direct. 'You're getting a smack. Come over here and get it now.'

Oh no.

I stayed put.

'Now,' she said, even louder. 'Make me come and get you and you'll get two.'

She meant what she said. I slowly edged her way. 'Soft?' I asked. 'Don't hit me hard.'

I tried to look cute. It didn't work.

'Ahhhh,' I screamed as the rubber sole turned into a whip and smacked into my bum.

'I'm sorry,' I cried. 'Sorry. Sorry. Sorry.'

'Have you learned your lesson?' she said. 'I don't want to have to do this again.'

I nodded. I didn't stop the hysterics until I got to my room.

I shut the door and went to the mirror.

Jeez!

My bum had a size six shoe imprint forming on it.

She got me good.

Yep. Little JT, growing up in Brisbane in the 1980s, could be a bugger ... surprise, surprise. I was as naughty as I was nice. And mostly I got what I deserved. Mum was the one to dish out the discipline. Oh, Dad had a big hand – huge – and it smacked me more than I would have liked, but mostly he was the threat and Mum was the reality. Mum would use Dad as a warning.

'Do you want me to get your father?' she would ask.

Duh.

The slipper only came out when I went too far. We don't smack kids these days, but back then it was part of raising a child.

So don't go calling child services, but, by all means, if you need some advice on slippers, give her a buzz.

Now let's get into my childhood: a tale of soft drinks, Space Invaders and, of course, Steeden footballs.

'Hey, Johnny, you want to be our ball boy?' Dad asked.

I looked at him and shook my head. 'Nup,' I said. 'I'm good.'

Why on earth would I want to spend my afternoon chasing footballs when I could be playing in the mud with my mates?

'I'll pay you a dollar,' he said. 'All you have to do is kick the football back.'

Now he had my attention.

How many cans of Fanta could I buy for a buck? Maybe 10. *Red frogs?* Like 100.

'OK,' I said. 'But you better pay up. And I'm going to spend it at the canteen after the game. Don't tell me I have to save it for a car or something stupid.'

My professional rugby league career began when I was four. I was employed as a ball boy for the Acacia Ridge Hotel A-grade rugby league team. I couldn't have cared less about football. I did it for soft drinks and sweets. Somewhere in Brisbane, on a suburban ground, this future Kangaroo picked up a football for the very first time because his dad offered him a dollar.

My father, Graeme Thurston, was an A-grade footy player. He played for Acacia Ridge Hotel and also another club called Browns Plains. And apparently, he was pretty good.

'Oh, he was a tough bugger,' one of his mates told me later. 'Real hard. I loved playing with him. When it was on, you wanted him by your side. I'm glad he was in my trench.'

Dad played a bit of hooker and also back row. He wasn't a big bloke, but what he lacked in size he made up for with heart. Apparently he would take anyone on. I can't remember too much of what he was like as a player, I was too busy chasing balls and thinking about how many red frogs I could buy with a buck. Other people have filled me in.

'Not a thing like you,' said another of his mates. 'Good, but a completely different player.'

So, that day when I was four, I pulled up my socks and positioned myself on the sideline. The referee blew his whistle; it was game on.

Whack!

A pair of giants collided. That must have hurt.

Crunch!

Another couple came together on the next play. It was brutal, and I loved it. The men were huge – well, they certainly looked that way to an all-skin-and-bone four-year-old – and they were smashing each other. It was violent, fast and loud.

Was it better than throwing mud at my mates?

Maybe ...

Soon the ball was hurtling towards the touchline. End over end, the football was a heat-seeking missile on a mission to take out the corner post. I would later find out it was called a grubber kick. But whatever, it was time to earn my buck. My little legs pumped as I ran down the field. I moved as fast as I could.

Oh no. That's going to end up on the highway.

But then, all of a sudden, it pulled up. The thick, wet grass – only the playing field had been mowed – stopped the ball dead.

Pheeewwww!

I didn't want to chase it over the fence. I picked it up and booted it back onto the field. And I reckon that was my very first rugby league kick.

I can't say I fell in love with rugby league right away – that didn't happen until I was about six. Until then it was all about spending the dollar Dad would give me, without fail after every match, at the canteen.

One ground had a Space Invaders machine, the old coffee-table type with the wooden base and glass top. Oh, how I loved that thing.

I would be on Dad as soon as the whistle went, my father exhausted, battered and bruised after his 80-minute war.

'Can you give the dollar to me in 20-cent coins?' I would ask.

He soon learned to keep small change.

I would then go and stack the coins on the top of the machine, and, one by one, they would disappear into its belly. Yep ... Space Invaders, soft drinks and sweets; that's how I discovered rugby league.

CHAPTER TWO

I WAS BORN INTO a big family. And when I say big, I mean *big*. My mum – Debbie Saunders – is one of 13. She has nine brothers and three sisters. So that means I have nine uncles, three aunties and a busload of cousins.

I am not real good at maths, so I am not going to count. But what I can tell you is that family has been a *big* part of my life. My childhood home was a brick three-bedder in Brisbane. Brand new when we moved in, it was a housing commission house on Commodore Street, Sunnybank Hills, in the southern suburbs of Brisbane. And it became a hub for family Thurston and Saunders.

With a *big* backyard, and an even *bigger* front yard, our house was the perfect place for a *big* family to get together. I can't remember a time when the house wasn't packed, jammed and almost bursting the bricks it was made of.

My early life was all barbecues, family and fun. Did I mention I had a *big* family?

They might as well have moved in; in fact, some of them did. The rest would come round every other day. And that is exactly how my mum wanted it. She is the glue that holds my family together.

We have had plenty of drama over the years: fights and fists. But Mum has always sorted it all out. Yeah, she is the boss. No doubt about it. Just ask her. But seriously, the old lady could put her foot down. And when she did we all listened.

Dad, a fitter and turner by trade, used to work long hours. He would leave before I woke up and get home after sunset. He also spent a lot of time on the road. But Mum was always home and we became inseparable. Later on she would go and work for the Queensland Police Force as a liaison officer up in Brisbane. But in the early days she was always there to give me a big fat hug whenever I needed one.

Or a smack with that slipper!

* * *

Being surrounded by people was my norm; I can't imagine growing up any other way. I have no doubt it made me the person I am today.

I was a second child. Both my mum and dad have children from previous marriages. I have an older brother, Robert, from Mum's first marriage. And I have an older sister, Katrina, from Dad's first marriage.

Dad emigrated from New Zealand – yeah, yeah, I'm half Kiwi – before I was born. Katrina and his former wife stayed in New Zealand. I didn't meet my sister until I was eight.

Robert lived between our house in Brisbane and his dad's in Melbourne. He is five years older than me, and, yes, we were always at each other. Mostly it would be over video games. We used to hire a Sega Master System in the holidays. Classic arcade games turned the lounge room into a war zone.

'Give me the control pad, Johnny,' Rob said. 'It's my go. You just died.'

I looked at him and smiled, before turning back to the screen.

To continue press X.

I pressed X.

'It's my go,' he yelled. 'You can't play again.'

Rob jumped up and moved his skinny little bum in front of the TV. I couldn't see a thing.

'Move,' I screamed. 'Get out of the way. You can play next.'

He wouldn't. So I threw the controller at his head.

'You're dead,' he screamed, his right foot powering forward to begin his charge.

I was off the moment the controller left my hand.

There were sliding doors leading from the lounge room to the backyard, and another set leading to the front yard. Mum always left both sets open because I had run into them once or twice. I went towards the doors leading to the front yard, and with a lightning step to the left I was through and out onto the patio.

Whack!

This time I stepped off my right foot, the evasive action stopping me from crashing into the privacy screen attached to the patio. I was heading full speed towards the tree.

Bang!

Another step, again a left. Now I was running circles around the gigantic trunk and, more importantly, around my brother.

'Sissy,' I yelled, the tree safely between him and me. 'You big girl.'

He suddenly stopped before changing direction.

Whoops!

I was now running straight towards him.

'Yeah?' he said, pinning me to the ground, knees buried in my chest. 'Let's see how hard a sissy can punch.'

For the record, it was *hard*. And that is where the Johnathan Thurston sidestep was born, the big left and the leaping right. My famous footballing footwork was developed out of necessity. Honed by a privacy screen and practised around a hulking tree as a means of avoiding a belting. Before evading defensive lines, I was evading my big brother. I had my own agility course in my backyard.

And it was as good as any I have seen in the NRL. We didn't need cones or hurdles; we had a clothesline, a gumtree and a privacy screen. The threat of being belted if caught was better than even the most demanding coach. I was always being chased, and sometimes I got caught.

‘Mum!’ I screamed. ‘Rob hit me. He chased me all the way down the street and belted me.’

Mum laughed. ‘Well, you should have run faster, son,’ she said.

I was a massive sook growing up.

‘Toughen up, princess,’ Mum would say. ‘You want to play with the big boys, then you’ll have to act like one.’

CHAPTER THREE

IT WAS PRETTY COOL when my little brother came along. I was so used to being the youngest that it was great to finally have someone I could boss around.

Shane was a tiny little kid, always the smallest in any group. And yeah, I belted him a couple of times. But I also looked after him. One of my jobs was to make sure he got to, and home from, school ...

'Mum!' I screamed. I was hysterical, tears rolling down my cheeks after catching the bus home. 'I've lost Shaney. He was there and then he wasn't. I can't find him anywhere.'

I was terrified. We were coming home from school and he just vanished; on the bus with me one minute, gone the next.

Mum laughed. 'Go and look inside,' she said.

And there he was, eating cereal, bum on the floor, watching cartoons. I ran up and punched him in the arm.

'What did you do that for?' he asked. 'You got off the bus and left me. The doors closed and I was on my own.'

Oh ...

I'd like to say I didn't lose him again, but I did.

Our home was the second house built on what would become a sprawling suburban estate. Surrounded by bush when we moved in, the suburb is now all roads, houses and families. But back then there was open space everywhere, and we put it to good use.

Sometimes it was cricket, mostly it was football, and when we had money for petrol it was a Yamaha PeeWee 50. Oh yeah. We rode that miniature motorbike until the tank ran dry.

The house was brick; it had three bedrooms, a lounge room and a kitchen. I never had my own room. I always shared, first with Micheal – more about my cousin in the next chapter – and then Shane. Sometimes it was both. We had bunk beds and it was first in, best dressed. Whoever went to bed first would claim whatever bunk they wanted, so I slept on both the top and the bottom. We were a family that shared everything.

I spent a fair bit of time in the living room. My little brother always had the run of the TV, so mostly we were watching *Gumby*, *Postman Pat* and *Fireman Sam*.

I was always last out of bed. By the time I got up Shane would already be eating his Weet-Bix while watching TV. We would sit there, mindless morning zombies, until Mum screamed at us to get ready for school.

'What are you two doing?' she would yell. 'We have to leave in two minutes.'

I didn't have a bedroom full of toys. There were no posters covering the walls. And there were no books on the shelves. No, my room was full of balls, bats and racquets. You had to be able to kick it, pass it or hit it – or I didn't want it.

We ended up getting an old TV in there a few years later. And then a Sega. Game on. We only ever used the bedroom for sleeping until we got that games system. And then we never left.

My bedroom was messy, there was rubbish everywhere. We would throw our clothes on the floor.

Dump our bats and balls in the corner. I don't think I cleaned it once. Sorry, Mum.

'Hey, Johnny,' Dad said, big smile on his face. 'Reckon you can score a try today?'

I shrugged.

'I'll give you a dollar if you can,' he said. My eyes lit up.

'In fact, I'll give you a dollar for every try that you score,' he continued. 'So you'll get three dollars if you can get three.'

I smiled. 'How much money you got?' I asked. He laughed, at least until the end of the game. I scored nine tries.

'You got a 10-dollar note?' I said, hand out the moment the full-time whistle was blown. There was barely a speck of dirt on my oversized black-and-white jersey.

'I'll owe you a dollar until I score next week.'

Dad gave me the ten. 'Just keep it,' he said. 'This was a one-time deal.'

Dad never offered me another incentive when it came to rugby league.

I played my first game of rugby league for Souths Acacia Ridge Junior Rugby League Football Club (JRLFC) when I was six. And apparently I was pretty good from the get-go.

I started playing football not long after one of my cousins came to live with us. Micheal Janson, my mother's nephew, moved into our house for a while when I was six. I am not sure why, but one day he was bunking down with me and it was great.

We all called Micheal 'Mickey Motor', and he fast became my best mate. He was right into his football and he ended up getting me into it too. He had already played a season with Souths and he wanted me to join him.

'Come and play with me, Johnny,' he said. 'We can be in the same team.'

Micheal was a year older but the 6s and 7s were combined. 'Yeah, righto,' I said. 'Beats watching you.'

Soon I was surrounded by footballs; my backyard was full of them. So too the front yard, the neighbour's yard and that ball-swallowing bush down the end of the street.

Yep. It was footy, footy and footy at the Thurston house. Seriously, we played so much we wore the grass out. With an endless supply of family that were both teammates and opponents, both front yard and back were reduced to tufts of green, swimming in baked, brown dirt.

My uncles never said no when I nagged them for a game. 'Righto,' Uncle Stephen would say. 'I'll go and get your other uncles too.'

Uncle Brett would be there, Uncle Phillip and Uncle Dean too. Sometimes we had enough to make it 13-on-13: a full-on international-rules match. And my uncles were mostly in their early twenties, full of energy and spark. We'd start the game. Back and forth, tries aplenty, and we'd still be going when the sun went down.

'Next try wins,' Uncle Stephen barked. 'Winner takes all.' He picked up the ball and started his run.

Did I mention that I was a bad loser? Yeah, I was a terrible sport. So my uncles would let me win. Well, most of the time.

I was waiting for Uncle Stephen to drop the ball, already thinking about my victory dance.

But Uncle Stephen was running. Fast.

What's he doing? He can't score. He always lets me win.

He burned down the sideline, a cheeky smile on his face, try line closing fast.

Surely he's going to drop it? Or just throw me an intercept?

He didn't. Uncle Stephen planted the ball and raised his arm towards the sky.

'Yeah, the trophy is mine,' he beamed. 'Last-minute try to win the grand final. Give me the Clive Churchill Medal now.'

And then I yelled. 'Na, next try wins,' I demanded. 'Game's not over. It's next try wins.'

But it wasn't. Uncle Stephen was already putting the imaginary Clive Churchill Medal around his neck.

Game over.

So I ran back home and bolted into the kitchen.

'I'm never playing with Uncle Stephen again,' I said to Mum, my eyes wet, my face red.

Whether it was cricket, football or the last jellybean in the jar, I had to win. The rough stuff didn't worry me a bit. I could take a beating, but only if I won. I was even worse when it came to cricket: I was never out.

'Na, I didn't knick it!' I would scream, even if the ball tore off a chunk of willow from the side of my self-scooped imitation Gray-Nicolls One Scoop. 'That's not out.'

I would throw the bat away in disgust when the decision wasn't overruled. And then, of course, I would go running to Mum.

'I love you, son,' she would say. 'But stop being a baby. Go on. Get back out there.'

CHAPTER FOUR

SO IT WON'T COME as a surprise that this mummy's boy had a cry on his first day of school. 'I don't want to go, Mum,' I said. 'I want to stay home with you.'

She gave me a hug and sent me on my way.

I was dropped at Acacia Ridge State School for my first day of school in a taxi. I have no idea whether or not it was because we didn't have a car. Maybe it was getting fixed. I am not sure, but I clearly remember both Mum and Dad taking me to school in a cab.

My first teacher was Mrs Shaw and I liked her a lot. Maybe she reminded me of Mum. Anyway, school ended up being OK.

All my report cards from primary school were good. I was hungry for information and did my work. I was never in trouble and, believe it or not, I would describe myself as a pretty good student, at least until I got to high school.

But ... I was also one of those kids who would have 'easily distracted and needs to choose his friends carefully' written in the comments section of his report.

Want to guess what my favourite subject was?

Yeah, you are right, it was sport. I liked class, but I loved recess and lunch because that was when we played sport, cricket in the summer, footy in the winter.

Later on, in Years 5 and 6, I got to play both cricket and football for the school. We would travel around taking on other schools and that was something I really enjoyed.

Have I told you that I was competitive?

Whack!

I hit it sweet, straight out of the meatiest part of the willow. I was running down the pitch, my eyes following the path of the ball. I was a Test cricketer in the making, an opening batsman, an opening bowler, and no doubt, on this day, on my way to scoring a ton.

Oh no!

I hadn't got as much on it as I thought. It was coming down and heading towards a pair of cupped hands.

Hands that belonged to a girl!

And *she* caught it.

I threw my bat down hard, before steaming off the field. I fancied myself as a bit of a cricketer. I loved it as much as footy. Maybe even more. And then a girl got me out.

I kicked the kit. I huffed and puffed. I don't think I spoke to anyone for the rest of the day. I just fumed. I walked over to Mum. I looked at her, waiting for her to say something to make me feel better.

She giggled.

So I went back and kicked the kit again.

I was into a bit of everything when I was young. It wasn't just footy and cricket. I also played a lot of snooker, table tennis and squash. If it had a ball, I was in.

I excelled in all forms of athletics. From the 100 metres to cross country, I pretty much won them all. I went to state level for both track and field. I think the only discipline I sucked in was shot put, but then again, the shot was heavier than me.

My best friend during primary school was my second

cousin Latoya. We started school together on the same day and got on from day dot.

Latoya's grandmother lived near our school. My mum and dad both worked late, so I would go back there and wait for them to pick me up. And yes, I probably played Barbie dolls with her, an experience that would come in handy later in life when I became father to three girls!

I had male friends too. Dusty Morton was one of my great childhood friends. My dad played footy with his father and we had a lot in common. We used to spend a lot of time together when our old men were playing footy or having a beer.

You probably know JT as a proud Aboriginal: a footballer who wears black, yellow and red boots to publicly acknowledge his heritage. But I was no Indigenous ambassador back in primary school; I was just a kid.

Seriously. I didn't even know what an Aboriginal was until I went to school. And even then, it meant nothing except for the fact that I was one. Well, in part ...

My mum is an Aboriginal, born and bred in Queensland. I started identifying myself as an

Aboriginal in primary school. I knew I had New Zealand heritage, but being so close to my uncles and cousins, and also living in Australia, I identified with Mum's side of the family tree. New Zealand was an ocean away. A nation we played in cricket and football. A place where a sister I had never met lived. I was an Australian Aboriginal.

And what did that mean?

Not a whole lot. I didn't know a thing about my family history. I can't even remember having a conversation about it until I was in my late twenties. And that probably wouldn't have happened had it not been for the introduction of the NRL All Stars match, which pitted an Indigenous team against a non-Indigenous one.

I guess I never asked about my cultural background because it was a non-issue. I was never discriminated against and I never encountered any serious form of racism. Plenty of Aboriginal kids went to my school at Acacia Ridge. Maybe that helped. All I know is that I was never disadvantaged because of the colour of my skin.

Lucky I didn't own up to being a Kiwi. Ha. Ha.

CHAPTER FIVE

I DIDN'T MIND SCHOOL, but I loved football. And my thing was scoring tries. I was small, even for a six-year-old. But I was fast. Real fast. Not many people could get hold of me once I caught the ball. I would take off towards the sideline and run the length of the field. Just ask Dad.

Scoring tries?

Yep, loved it. *Tackling?*

Not so much.

I was a tiny fella and I struggled to pull the big boys down. Thankfully, I didn't have to do much 'D' when I was young because I played on the wing.

But I had a go. I might have been tiny, but I was tough. Thanks to my dad, my brothers and my uncles, I was used to coping a hit. I was always getting roughed up and never short of a bruise.

My first real memories of playing are from when I moved to Souths Sunnybank JRLFC when I was eight. I went to that club because one of my dad's best mates had a son who played for them. His name was Josif Mladenovic.

We were as thick as thieves. We hung out not only at the footy club, but also at my house and his. Kick after kick, pass after pass, we became inseparable. Yep. Long before JT and Darren Lockyer, JT and Cooper Cronk, and JT and Michael Morgan, it was JT and Josif ...

One day Josif had an idea. 'Why don't you just stand out there,' he said, pointing to the sideline. 'I can just do a big pass and you can run to the line without anyone touching you. All the tacklers stand in the middle of the field.'

So that's what I did. Josif grabbed the ball at first receiver and threw a perfect spiral pass, hitting me right on the chest. I looked up and there was nobody in front of me. I sprinted my way to the line – not that I needed to rush with all the defenders still in the middle – and scored the easiest try of my career.

'Yeah, let's do that all the time,' I said to Josif. 'I don't really like being tackled.'

Josif was a really good football player. He played in the halves and I played on the wing. And we were just nine when we started thinking structures and plans. Josif was a great passer and talker. I was fast. So every set he would run a couple of forwards before throwing a long ball out to me. And I am talking a 15-metre pass.

I always positioned myself so I was in space. He would get the ball to me, out front and on my chest. From there it was easy. I would just run and score. And looking back I am pretty amazed that we were running structured sets in Under 8s. We didn't lose a game for three years.

I kicked my first proper goal during my first year with Souths: it had been drop kicks until we moved up into the Under 8s. It was early morning, the grass drenched with dew. The surface was as slippery as an ice-skating rink, as cold as one too. My bare feet were numb; we didn't wear boots until we were 10.

I built a little sandcastle to place the ball on. I had no idea what I was doing but I had seen it done on TV. I stuck the ball on top after eyeing off the little posts made from PVC pipe. I walked back and moved in.

Whack!

I got it. I struck the ball pretty well from the start; I can't remember missing many. I guess I had a fair bit of natural talent.

My first pair of footy boots came from Kmart: a pair of budget black Trax. I got them when we moved into the 10s and were allowed to wear boots. I thought they were brilliant. It was like strapping on a Superman cape, but instead of flying they gave me footballing powers: the step, the skip and the speed.

They were black with moulded rubber studs. And I loved them; I might have even taken them to bed and cuddled them like a teddy bear. I would score a lot of points in them before wearing them out. My feet didn't grow a lot back then so I had them until they were ruined.

We always watched the footy when it was on. Dad, the brothers, the uncles and me. We would all pile into the lounge room and watch the match of the day on our old-school TV, a square screen buried in a hefty wooden box.

The first season of top-grade footy I can remember is 1989. I watched rugby league before that but I didn't really know what was going on. Mum was a Canberra Raiders fan so I followed them too. Dad went for the Bulldogs and so did my brother; it created some fun. It was always mayhem when the Dogs played the Raiders. We would get right into it.

Supporting the Raiders ended up being a pretty good move – Canberra were an incredible side in the early 1990s. There was Mal Meninga (big Mal), Laurie Daley (Loz), Ricky Stuart (Sticky) and Steve Walters. They were a side with talent to burn. And they won a lot more games than they lost.

Mal was always my favourite, all tree-trunk legs and palms of steel. He was so big. I was tiny and was completely in awe of his size. I used to love watching him trample blokes. I used to imagine that it was me running over the top of defenders, left arm in a cast, scoring under the posts.

Fair to say Mal was my first idol. Later it was Allan Langer, Darren Lockyer (Locky) and then Andrew Johns (Joey).

Origin was my favourite type of football. It was a huge occasion in the Thurston house. We would always throw a party and the house would be full of colour and noise. And we hated New South Wales.

So did I dream of becoming a State of Origin star? You betcha.

CHAPTER SIX

'NOT YET, DAD!' I SCREAMED. 'Just one more kick.'

He stood next to the car, shaking his head. 'One,' he shouted back. 'Or you'll be walking home. It's already dark.'

Dad knew there was no such thing as 'one more' when it came to rugby league and me. He would soon be dragging me from Jim Murdoch Oval – the home of Souths Sunnybank JRLFC – by my filthy jersey.

I had stayed back after training to practise my chip and chase. With everyone in my team long gone, the floodlights burning bright and the senior teams running riot, I had claimed a corner of the ground for myself.

I turned away from Dad and went back to work.

OK. This time I'll get it right ...

'Noooo,' I yelled, the ball disobeying me once again.

I had imagined the perfect landing, visualised success. I had willed it once it was in the air.

'Ahhhhh!' I yelled, this time loud enough for the Under 19s to stop mid-drill and see what the skinny little kid in the corner was screaming about. I ignored them and raced towards the ball, now at rest and about 15 metres from where I had wanted it to land.

Whack!

I launched the badly bouncing football over the fence, kicking it as hard as I could. This time it went exactly where I had aimed.

Whoops!

Now I had to go and get it. I jumped the fence.

'Why?' I growled, ball back in my hand. 'Why won't you just bounce back?'

For hours I had been attempting to pull off the perfect chip and chase: a short kick that you are meant to regather after it goes over the defensive line. Kicking for yourself, it should bounce back into your arms after you run through the opposition line.

Yeah ... should. I couldn't get the ball to bounce back to me after I kicked it, no matter how hard I willed it to, no matter what I tried.

'Righto!' I screamed back at Dad, who was now beeping the horn. 'Just one more.'

I turned my attention to the ball, no longer enemy but friend. 'Sorry, I shouldn't have kicked you over the fence,' I said. 'You just need to do the right thing. Please, just bounce back.'

I slowly started my run, positioning the ball while on the move. I dropped it, making sure its path to my foot was straight and true. And then I carefully kicked.

'Damn it!' I yelled.

The ball darted off to the right as soon as it hit the turf.

I was lucky my mum couldn't hear my language. I chased the ball down and kicked it straight in the guts. 'Have fun on the road. I hope you get hit by a truck.'

I slammed the door when I finally got into the well-warmed-up car.

'Keep at it, son,' Dad said. 'You'll get it. Practice makes perfect.'

I sat silent, stewing all the way home. Soon we were in the driveway, a turn of a key killing the engine.

'Dad,' I said, 'can you get me a new ball?'

* * *

I was obsessed with football by the time I was 10. I would stay after training, kicking and passing, until the lights went off, or until Dad put me on his shoulder and threw me in the car. I was there every day, chipping, charging and, when things didn't work out, chasing the ball over the fence.

I was always practising, whether in the backyard or at the ground, with my uncles, my brothers, with Josif, or by myself. I would pass, bomb, grubber and chip.

Oh boy, did I chip!

I spent months attempting to master that chip and chase. Hour after hour, day after day, I went out onto that field and willed the ball to come back to me. It refused to behave. The ball was bouncing forward, or to the side, and sometimes even stopping dead. It did everything except bounce back into my hands.

Then, suddenly and from nowhere, came an idea, a light bulb flashing inside my head.

Maybe it's how you're holding the ball.

I had spent all my time worrying about how I was *kicking* the football, not how I was holding it. I looked at the ball and leant it forward in my hands. I had previously been tilting it back. I stuck my foot into it and ran.

Please ... Please ...

The ball bounced and rocketed straight back into my chest. I gave the ball a big kiss before planting it on the ground to score an imaginary try.

Maybe it was a lucky bounce?

It wasn't.

The next ball bounced straight back in my hands. So did the one after that. In fact, they all did, only Dad and his horn stopping the unrelenting procession of short kicks and running catches. And that is how I have chip-kicked ever since. It pretty much always bounces back – not forward, not to the side, and it doesn't stop dead.

Most of the things I do on a football field have been learned through experimentation and persistence. I taught myself all of these things because I was obsessed with being able to do everything. If I saw a player doing something on TV that I couldn't do, well, it was all 'just one more, Dad' and kicking balls onto the road until I could to it.

That is just how I was.

And I was like that with most things. If I couldn't do something, I would keep on trying until I could.

CHAPTER SEVEN

ALLAN LANGER WAS PARTLY responsible for the fact that I grew up with a football firmly tucked under my arm.

'Alfie' was really big in the early 1990s and he is a guy I spent a lot of time both watching and copying. I would go out to the backyard and attempt to replicate what he did on a football field.

Langer changed the way rugby league players kicked a football. He made the football do things that didn't seem possible. He could get the ball to break to the left or to the right after hitting the ground. He could make it run or stop dead. He could also move the football in the air.

Sometimes he would hold the ball flat, hands on each end, and kick it square in the belly. The ball would wobble along the ground like a grenade. It was a nightmare for fullbacks to clean up.

It was magic, and because of Langer, I wanted to be a magician. Alf had all sorts of kicks in his bag of tricks and I watched, paused, rewound and replayed in a bid to learn some of them. So yeah, there were plenty more horn blasts and balls sent over the fence.

I remember spending months trying to get the ball to bend once I had kicked it. At training I would use the goalposts. At home it was the clothesline first, and then the gumtree. I would hit the ball with different parts of my foot to see what reaction I could get out of it. I would also change the way I held it, hoping for a result.

And, just like the chip, I eventually got it right.

I can't blame Alfie entirely for making me live with a football. Others, including Ricky Stuart, Laurie Daley and Mal Meninga, had plenty to do with shaping my game too.

The 1990s were a great time to be learning how to play rugby league. During that era the game was being reinvented. Guys like Langer and Stuart were doing things that had never been done before. Stuart's long passing game had never been seen before in rugby league.

Stuart began his career as a rugby union player and he brought his long spiral cut-out with him. I used to watch hours and hours of these guys play on tape. They were my first coaches in a way. I threw countless long balls like Ricky and was always trying to be like Alf.

I was pretty much just a running footballer until I was 13. My strength was my speed. Life on the wing was good. I was scoring more tries than I made tackles. But soon I wanted more. I suppose I needed a challenge.

That first challenge came with my passing game. I was pretty good at throwing a ball on my natural side: right-to-left, but my left-to-right was poor. I could only do what they call a floater, which is a flat pass with no revolutions on the ball. You hold the ball at six o'clock and release it, towards your target, when you get to nine o'clock.

I could also spiral the footy when passing right to left, not a problem. I could hit my mark and throw it a good 15 metres. But going the other way, well, I couldn't throw it far at all. I would have to cut the distance with my feet, run the ball to my target instead of using the air. You could get away with doing that if you had to, and most did. It was a lot easier to hide a weakness than to confess to having one, let alone fix it. For me it was a problem because I wanted to be able to do everything.

The solution smacked me in the chest. Literally.

I was playing a game at school when I was hit with the longest, fastest and hardest left-to-right spiral I had ever caught.

'How did you do that?' I asked Russell, the guy who threw the perfect pass.

He shrugged. 'I'm left-handed,' he said. 'That's my good side.'

'Can you show me?' I asked. 'Just do it real slow.'

And he did. I watched on as his left hand took control of the ball. With his palm he took the top belly of the ball, and with his wrist he flicked it towards him. His right hand held the ball underneath, gripping it with his thumb and his index finger: that was the hand that pushed the ball to the target. But it was his left that did most of the work.

'Again,' I said.

And he did: over and over and over and over again until he realised I wouldn't stop asking for more.

I went home, grabbed the footy and tried to replicate what I had seen. I sat on the lounge and ripped at the ball with my left hand, making it spin back towards my chest. I then practised the shove with the right. Then I put it all together.

Soon I was out in the backyard hitting targets: first at five metres, then 10 and finally 15.

And I threw them at training too, despite the real risk of spraying a pass into the fence. But I wasn't embarrassed when one slipped – the training paddock is where you train. That is where you are supposed to make your mistakes.

Looking back, I don't know why I was identifying my weaknesses at such a young age. And I certainly don't know how I came up with the drills to turn them into strengths. Maybe it comes back to that competitive streak? Maybe it is a bit of OCD? You decide.

CHAPTER EIGHT

AS MY SKILLS IMPROVED, so did my football. I became a bit of a utility as I moved into my teenage years. I went from being a try-scoring winger to playing anywhere in the backline. I still liked scoring tries – certainly more than tackling – but I was soon doing more of the latter than the former.

I was moved into the centres when I was 11. I also played the odd game at No. 6. My game was still very much reliant on speed, but I was slowly learning how to use the ball and my body to set up others in attack, and my shoulders to bring them down in defence.

I didn't lose a game until I was 13. Winning came part and parcel with playing. It was all too easy. And then they moved us up a division.

Oh. Maybe we're not so good.

It was the reality check both the team and I needed – we were cruising until then. It is a cliché, but you learn more about yourself from a defeat than a victory. And we lost plenty in the 13s. Sometimes you need to be beaten to want to improve. You don't have the motivation to get better if you think you are already the best.

Personally, I worked hard on my defence. I was always a small guy and tackling never came naturally. I would rely on my speed to bring them down. I would let them get into a position that suited me, and then use my pace to get to them.

I always went in low; I never went in looking for huge contact. I would use their momentum to get them down. I never attempted to drive and use my weight, and with good reason: I weighed a smidge more than nothing.

I would have been bumped straight to the ground if I had attempted to go high and straight-on. So I didn't. I hit them low, still hard, and let them fall back over my shoulder. Oh yeah, I would have to hold on for dear life and hope it was enough.

And mostly it was.

* * *

I made my first rep team when I was 12. I was selected for the Queensland primary schools team when I was in Year 7. I had to make the district side first, then the regional side, and ultimately I was picked for the Queensland team. I was pretty excited because the state carnival was an away trip. Until that point I had only ever been out of Brisbane once or twice, and that was down the road to the Gold Coast with the family.

And guess where the carnival was held? Townsville: my future home.

I had never been on a plane before. And I was scared. My brother had been on a plane – he went to Sydney once with Mum – so I quizzed him. 'Will it crash?' I asked. 'Is it safe? Will I get sick? You know those bags they have ... they're for spew, yeah?'

I was sweating when I put my seatbelt on.

'Excuse me,' I said to the flight attendant. 'I don't think this belt is tight enough.'

She looked down and it was already strangling my waist. 'It's fine, sweetie,' she said. 'Don't worry. Everything will be OK.'

It did little to reassure me.

My brother Shane had given me a challenge before I got on. He told me that the plane goes so fast when it takes off that it pins you back into your seat. He told me you can't pull your head from the seat. So I made a game out of it and tried to lean forward as the plane began its takeoff. I had to accept defeat on my first attempt, the plane winning.

We arrived in Townsville a couple of hours later. I had no idea that this place would eventually become my home. All I could remember about Townsville then is the Willows Shopping Centre and the heat. It was winter but it was still hot.

We ended up playing a bunch of games, and the week ended with me earning my first ever Queensland jersey. I was picked for the state side and handed a maroon jumper. I beamed with pride when I put it on for the very first time. I imagined it was the real deal: a Queensland State of Origin jersey. I felt invincible.

And that is the moment my lifelong rivalry with New South Wales began.

We played the NSW schools side in a three-match series. I went into my first Queensland camp that week too. We spent the week in Warwick, south-west of Brisbane. It was the middle of winter and it was proper freezing. I wasn't happy because they made us all go to a local school during the day and do schoolwork. How dare they! I thought it was all going to be football, but we only trained in the afternoon.

My parents came to watch when we finally got on the field. So did a bunch of my uncles and family friends. Again I felt like a star. I was wearing a Queensland jersey and a whole mob of family had travelled across the state just to watch me play.

And you will be happy to know, at least if you are a Queenslander, that my domination over New South Wales began from the get-go. We won the series.

Go the Maroons!

CHAPTER NINE

FAST-FORWARD TWO YEARS AND I'm being dragged out of the backseat of the family car.

'I'll just stay here,' I said. 'It's too hot. You go and I'll wait in the car.'

The summer sun had scorched away the green and turned my local footy ground brown. The soft spring grass was now like hard, compacted straw.

'Come on,' Mum said. 'Get out. Go and have a kick with the boys.'

I looked out the window and the ground was packed. From toddlers to teenagers, boys were running, passing and kicking. Footballs were flying.

'Na, you go,' I said to Mum. 'You take Shaney and I'll stay here.'

Mum shook her head. 'But you have to sign on. If you don't register today you won't be able to play.'

I shrugged my shoulders and shut the door. I didn't care if I never played rugby league again. And it was all over a tracksuit.

'Hey, look at Dane,' one of the boys had said at a football carnival the year before. 'What's he wearing?'

I turned and looked towards a kid walking into the clubhouse, bag hanging from his right shoulder. His name was Dane Campbell. He was one of the kids in the team we were about to play.

'Is that Broncos gear?' another kid in my team asked.

It was. Dane was covered from head to toe in the maroon, yellow and white of the Brisbane Broncos. Wearing an oversized jacket made of that parachute-type material. He had oversized full-length pants to match. He was also wearing a Broncos polo and had a Broncos bag.

'Wow,' said one of the boys. 'He must be good.'

Not that good. I'm better than him, I thought.

'He must have been signed by the Broncos,' said someone else. 'He's on his way.'

I was 13 when I first saw a kid wearing a Brisbane Broncos tracksuit – and boy, did it drive me crazy!

Why has he got one? Where's my tracksuit? I'm better than him.

This Dane kid could play, in fact he would go on to play in the NRL for the Knights, but he was no better than me. The only thing he had that I didn't was size. He was a big unit and I was a skinny little thing.

Soon everyone seemed to have a Broncos tracksuit. Well, everyone except me. There they all were, walking around in their shiny new gear, chests puffed out and looking a million bucks. And there I was, slumped in a corner wearing a dirty old Rip Curl jumper. The Broncos started handing out scholarships when I was 13. And by the time I was 15 every decent player I knew had a Broncos tracksuit in their wardrobe.

But not me.

Despite making every representative team I could, I had never even spoken to anyone connected with the Broncos. And boy, did it make me angry.

The Broncos were the team I wanted to play for. My love-hate affair with the Broncos began in 1988 when they were born. Until then Queensland didn't have their own team in the NSWRL – the best rugby league competition in Australia – and everyone in Brisbane was forced to support a side from either New South Wales or the ACT.

Everything changed in 1988 when the Brisbane Broncos were formed. Suddenly Queensland had its own side. And it seemed like everyone in Queensland except for me switched to support the Broncos. I loved Mal, Ricky and Loz so I kept on supporting Canberra.

But it was difficult for me because Brisbane were a juggernaut. In 1993, just five years after they were formed, their average home crowd was 43,200. That is the biggest average crowd in the history of rugby league. And it is no wonder when they had a side that included Langer, Steve Renouf, Kevin Walters, Julian O'Neill, Glenn Lazarus, Trevor Gillmeister and a young Wendell Sailor to name a few. They went on to win their second premiership that year, beating St George 14–6. So even though I didn't support them, I wanted to play for them.

And that is why being looked over for a tracksuit hurt me to my core. I would have traded my entire collection of Air Jordans, my video games, and maybe even my little brother for one!

But the only side that showed any interest in me was the South Queensland Crushers. At some point I was invited to have a look at their set-up. I was impressed, but for whatever reason nothing ever came of it. I couldn't even get a look-in with Brisbane's second team. No one would be interested in me for another five years.

Yep. No one.

I kept on making all the rep teams but no NRL team would even talk to me.

Nothing.

I started getting really frustrated. I didn't know why I was being overlooked. At no point did I question my ability. I knew I was good enough. I considered myself a better player than most of the kids who were being signed, and that is what upset me. I was still small, but that wasn't stopping me from outperforming them on the field.

It was about then that I met a bloke called Cameron Smith (Smithy). I had been playing against Cameron since I was 13. He played for Logan Brothers and was part of a really good side. We spoke for the first time at a tryout for an Under 14s Brisbane team.

'G'day,' he said, hand outstretched. 'I'm Cameron.' I shook his hand. 'Johnny,' I said.

And that was how we met. 'What do you play?' I asked. 'Halfback,' he replied. 'And you?' 'No. 9,' I said.

Yep. That's right. I had been picked as a hooker and Cameron Smith as a half. Ha.

CHAPTER TEN

CAMERON AND I WERE soon on a training field, preparing for our trial. We had been put into the same group for a defensive drill. I looked him up and down. We were going to be tackling each other and I thought I had him covered.

Whack!

I was on my back. Hurting.

Heck! What is this guy made of? Steel?

I felt like I had just been hit by a truck. And it got worse once I was on the ground. Smithy locked my knees together and threatened to rip me in half.

'Man, what are you doing?' I said, still lying in the dirt. 'This is just training.'

He simply offered a smile.

I soon learned that this Cameron Smith guy did

everything at 110 per cent. He never cut a corner and went as hard as he could, all the time and every time.

And I also learned that he was deceptively strong. He wasn't much to look at, but after being hit just once I knew he was as tough as any front-row forward. He was all elbows and knees, wiry muscle and granite-hard bone. He was stronger than any bloke our age.

I made a mental note.

Don't ever end up in a group with him again.

I also decided that this was a guy I wanted to play with instead of against. I would get my opportunity …

But still I couldn't get that Broncos tracksuit. And it was really getting me down.

Things weren't much better at home. One of my neighbours was making my life hell. I was playing a game of backyard cricket with my brother when I whacked one.

Sheesh!

The ball went straight over the fence.

My neighbour was in his backyard watering his lawn. 'You lose a ball?' he asked, with a smile.

I nodded.

'You want it back?' he asked. I nodded again.

‘Well, you’re welcome to come get it,’ he said. ‘Come on, jump over. You’ll have to find it. My eyes aren’t so good. I think it went in the garden.’

I walked over to the fence: rows of greying wood, nailed to beams with rusted nails. I jumped up and hooked my fingers over the tops of the fence palings. My brother pushed at my feet, launching me with a boost.

Whoosh!

A metal bar flew through the air the moment before my brother sent my head towards the sky.

Whack!

The bar crashed into a paling, wood splintering and then smashing, inches from my face. The neighbour had taken a swing at me with a metal bar. He would have hit me in the head had my brother lifted me a moment earlier.

This guy was a nuisance. Seriously. Every time a ball would go over the fence, he would want to rip my head off. He would scream and yell. One time I kicked a plastic football over the fence. Soon his little head was looking at me.

‘You want this back, boy?’ he said, holding up the football. I nodded.

He then jammed a knife into the ball. 'Well, forget it,' he said, but they weren't the exact words he used. He was much less polite.

My neighbour had no idea that one of my dad's A-grade mates was sitting in the backyard, watching it all.

'No!' Dad's mate screamed. 'You didn't just swear at a kid and stab his ball!'

Dad's mate jumped the fence and chased him towards the house. He was ready to knock some sense into him. Lucky for my neighbour, he made it inside in the nick of time. Door safely locked, he called the cops.

We didn't get many balls back once they went over that fence. We ended up banning bombs up that end of the yard while playing footy. And when it came to cricket, it was most definitely six and out.

Soon summer was coming to an end and it was time to play football. Or was it?

Mum looked down at me, her face as sad as it was angry. 'Get out of the car now,' she said. 'You'll cook to death in there. It's an oven.'

I was already starting to sweat, the air a February furnace.

I would be medium–well-done in 20 minutes.

'OK but I'm not going to sign up,' I said. 'I don't want to play.'

Dad had his turn. 'Don't be stupid, son,' he said. 'You love footy.'

No. I used to love footy.

'Maybe I'll just have a year off,' I said. 'I'll see how I go. I'll probably come back.'

That was a lie. I had no intention of playing rugby league again. It wasn't that I didn't like football. It was just I didn't think anyone was going to give me an opportunity to make a future out of it. I had dreamed of becoming an NRL player my entire life and now it seemed like an impossible dream. I had put so much into it and had got nowhere.

My coach was great, I loved the boys in the team, but I had just had my fill. I wanted to go and hang out with my friends. I didn't want to spend another year watching players I was better than walking around like kings in their Broncos gear.

'OK,' Dad said, 'but why don't you have a chat to a couple of people first? It's a pretty big decision. And I think it's the wrong decision.'

He dragged me up to the clubhouse and sat me down with the club president, Adrian Griffin.

'Mate, you have plenty of talent,' he said. 'You could go all the way. I understand you're frustrated, but I reckon you could regret this in a few months.'

I wasn't listening.

'Why don't we just sign you up?' he said. 'You don't have to play but if you change your mind, you can. If you don't sign now, that's it. You want to be able to play later if you decide you want to. The paperwork has to go in now.'

I had no intention of playing but this would keep Mum and Dad happy. I signed on the dotted line.

Thank goodness!

Of course I ended up changing my mind and I played that year. But I wouldn't have if not for the advice of Mum, Dad and Adrian Griffin. I can honestly say my rugby league career could have ended there and then. I wouldn't be here today, writing this, had I not signed on to play Under 15s.

CHAPTER ELEVEN

THIS IS THE PART OF my story that I didn't want to tell. A chapter I am not proud of and part of my life I wish I could change.

In telling my story I considered skipping over this part of my life. It certainly would have been easier to leave it out of this book. But this is part of my story. These things happened. And I feel I owe you the truth.

The mistakes I have made in my life have helped shape me into the person I am today as much as the things I got right. Before I got to the top I was at the bottom. I have spent much of my life trying to be good to make up for the bad.

I hope the following confessions can do some good. If just one kid reads this and is inspired to make a life-changing choice, I will be glad to have told you about the bad that went along with the good.

I also want to say sorry to the people I have hurt. I can't stand the thought that people out there may think that I am a fake. That I am not the person I am publicly portrayed to be because of some of the things I did in the past. I'm sorry. And I can promise you I am not the person I was back then. Now to the tough part ...

It began with a bottle of rum and a bunch of mates. We went to the bottle shop with a fistful of coins and paid a guy to go in and buy us a bottle of rum. We mixed it with Coke and drank the entire bottle.

I was 13. That was the first time I got drunk. We downed the booze in a park and went to a party. I was sick the next day, my first hangover. I couldn't remember what we had done or how I got home. I said I would never drink again.

But we were standing outside the very same bottle shop the very next week. Soon we had another of bottle of rum and we were back at the park. Another party. Another hangover. This would become my standard Saturday night for the next two years.

Then things got worse. Sometimes there were no parties. Sometimes we wouldn't be let in. Or sometimes they would finish before we were ready to go home. So we would hit the street.

'Over there, Johnny,' one of my mates said. 'That Hilux. It'll be easy to get into.'

He was right. The Hilux was an older car. It didn't have an alarm and the lock was low-tech. I slowly walked my way towards the 4WD parked on a dark street, all quiet, all the residents fast asleep. I pulled out my screwdriver: a flathead with a yellow handle. I paused and looked up and down, left and right. Nothing. No one. All clear. So I jammed the metal end of the tool into the lock and reefed it left.

Pop!

I winced as the metal broke, the noise startling both me and my mates.

'We're good,' said my mate.

No house lights had come on. The street was still dark and empty. I opened the door.

Click!

I winced again. In the dead silence of night the latch cracked like a thunderclap. I had another look around. Nothing. No one. All clear. So I stuck my head into the car and went straight for the glove box. I opened it up and stuck my hand in. I found only papers. No sunglasses. No wallets. Nothing I could sell.

I was backing my way out of the car when something caught my eye. It was a bit of metal, lit up by the streetlight. I stuck my hand down and grabbed it before giving it a shake.

Ching! Ching!

It was a moneybox. I grabbed it and left the car. 'Let's go,' I said. 'Quick.'

We turned and sprinted. Legged it all the way down the street and around the corner. We didn't stop running until we were in another suburb. We opened the box in an alleyway behind a shop.

'What's in it, Johnny?' said one of my mates. 'What did we get?'

I ripped off the lid. 'Take a look at this!' It was full of money. It took us five minutes to count it all. 'That's over $2500,' I said.

We lived like kings for the next two weeks. New clothes, new shoes and rum: the good stuff for a change.

We started with sheds. There were four of us in my group and we would go out together on Saturday nights.

We would walk the streets with a footy and look for a house with the lights out. We would kick the footy over the fence and go and knock on the door to ask for it back. If no one answered we would jump the fence. And then we would break into the shed.

We were after lawnmowers and whipper snippers. We got $120 for a working lawnmower and $80 for a good whipper snipper. One of my mates knew an older fella who would come round and buy them from us.

We started with sheds and ended up moving on to cars.

I would always carry a screwdriver in my pocket.

We had a few run-ins with the cops. We were chased a few times after being sprung but we outran them every time. They were always stopping us too. We couldn't go a night without having them stop us for a once-over.

I won't name any of the guys I got into strife with but they are still mates of mine today. And believe it or not they all made it out the other side. They all got through school and ended up learning a trade. They are all successful in their own right now and some of the best blokes you could ever meet. We were never bad people. We just did bad things.

My football really suffered during this period. How could it not have? Late nights and drinking. Needless to say, I wasn't focused on football at all. I was also getting into trouble at school, at least when I was there. I didn't show up on most days. I think I might have even been suspended.

I am not proud of any of this. To be honest I feel terrible just thinking about it. But I can't hide from it. These were my mistakes and my mistakes alone. I can't blame my mates, I can't blame my family and I can't blame my cultural heritage. I had a fantastic upbringing and the things I did were no reflection on my parents or anybody else. Mum and Dad would have killed me had they known.

I was young and I was stupid. And now that I am older, and a role model to some, I hope others won't make my mistakes. And for anyone heading down the wrong path, remember it is never too late to change your life. Work out what you want to be or do and go for it.

I was 15 when I understood that my behaviour was going to stop me from realising my dream of becoming an NRL player.

So I decided to change my life ...

CHAPTER TWELVE

UNCLE DEAN GOT ME an interview at St Mary's College, Toowoomba. I was halfway through Year 10 and my life was a mess.

'You'll end up in jail, son, if you keep on this path,' Uncle Dean said. 'You need a change of lifestyle. I think you need to move away from Brisbane and the blokes you're getting into trouble with. I think going to Toowoomba will sort you out.'

I nodded. He was right. I knew my life had to be turned around. I was never going to become an NRL player if I was locked away for stealing cars.

The principal of St Mary's looked me straight in the eye. 'So you want to turn your life around?' he asked. 'Well, this is the place for you. I can promise you that we'll help you get to where you want to be. But you have to want it.'

I was sitting in an oversized chair, palms sweating, Uncle Dean by my side.

'Of course he wants to,' Uncle Dean replied on my behalf, speaking matter-of-factly to Bob White, the principal. Gary Reen, the coach of the football team, was also at the meeting. 'And he's going to.'

Reen turned to me. 'Is that right?' he asked. I nodded.

'Well, your grades aren't good enough,' he said, 'so you can show me how much you want to be here by going back to Brisbane and improving your marks. If you can get up to a satisfactory standard then we'll have a place for you here.'

I wasn't sure I could improve my grades; I was a struggling student.

'Maybe I should just leave school at the end of the year,' I said to Mum when I got back to Brisbane. 'I could finish up Year 10 and go and get an apprenticeship. I don't need school. Maybe I can become an electrician.'

'Like hell you will,' she blasted. 'You're going to that school whether you like it or not. Now go back to your old school and fix your grades. Do it or else there'll be hell to pay.'

So that's what I did. With Mum's hell-or-high-water demand, I started turning up to all my classes and I paid as much attention as I could. And instead of drinking, smoking and stealing, I studied.

I worked hard and improved my grades. I had a big smile on my face the next time I sat down in that oversized chair, palms sweat-free as they held onto the best report I'd ever had.

'OK, we just have to find you someone to stay with,' said the principal. 'And a football team to play for. Ever heard of the Toowoomba All Whites? I'll set you up.'

Uncle Dean beamed when I gave him the news. 'That's great, Johnny,' he said. 'This will be the best move you ever make.'

And it was. It would be the move that stopped me from taking the wrong path. And I can't thank Uncle Dean enough. He not only got me the interview but also paid my tuition fees. Uncle Dean knew I needed help and he was willing to give me whatever he could. He knew the only way to save me was to get me out of Brisbane.

So I moved to Toowoomba a kid on a mission. I was finally ready to get serious about football. I was going to leave all my baggage in Brisbane and clean up my life so I could become the best footballer I could be. I was excited by the prospect of going to St Mary's. It wasn't just going to be good for me as a person but also as an athlete, because it was a rugby league school.

I would be playing for a strong school team that was watched closely by scouts from the NRL and would get an opportunity to impress.

I moved in with the Seddons – a great family who welcomed me into their home as if I was their own. They had a nice suburban house in Toowoomba and I was given everything I needed: a room, a bed, food and an instant family. The Seddons were rugby league people too. Their son Eugene was a good player who had trialled with South Sydney just before I got there.

That was the first time I realised that there was a world outside of the Broncos. I had always thought that it was Brisbane or nothing. But when I moved in with the Seddons I realised there were another 15 teams out there and all I needed was one of them to give me a start.

Easy, right? Ha.

Anyway, I now had a light at the end of the tunnel. I still believed I was better than everyone else, but now

I had the motivation to prove it. I was ready to make the most of my fresh start.

Luckily my new mates weren't into the same things that got me into trouble in Brisbane. It was a different lifestyle. Sure, the guys I met through school and footy would go to parties and muck around but it was child's play compared to what I had been doing in Brisbane.

Mum checked up on me regularly. She was relentless. 'Are you being a good boy, Johnny?' she would ask. 'You better not be getting into trouble. I'll come down and belt you all the way back to Brisbane if you muck up.'

And she meant it. Mum kept tabs on me with phone calls to the school, the Seddons and my new footballing friends. Mum also came to see me on most weekends. She would make the two-hour trip with Uncle Dean. I had plenty of support.

Now I was ready to go to the next level. I was 16 when I arrived and I was put straight into an Under 17s team at the Toowoomba All Whites. It was then that I made my full-time switch to the halves.

I hit the ground running and things moved pretty fast. The All Whites were a great club and I was playing with good players. Still, I was a little surprised when

I was selected to play for Queensland in the Under 17s State of Origin team. I can't remember much about that match. The only thing that really stands out is the fact they didn't pick Cameron Smith. I was completely gobsmacked by the omission. Smithy was the best hooker in the state by a mile. I couldn't work out why he had been brushed.

Anyway, the game was at Lang Park and I must have done OK because I ended up being signed by a manager.

High-profile player agent Sam Ayoub got in touch with my mum after the carnival and told her he was interested in taking me on. He took my parents out to dinner in Brisbane and said he wanted to become my agent.

Why? I still have no idea.

Nobody had ever shown even the slightest interest in me. Player managers were at all my games by the time I was 13. They were jumping on players, pen in one hand and contract in the other. Always on the lookout for the next big thing, they would also go out and visit the players' parents, telling them how good their sons were and where they could take them. But no one was interested in me.

Until Sam came along. He had some pretty big clients. He managed Queensland legends like Jason Smith and Adrian Lam. I had seen him at games and I knew who he was. And I had no hesitation putting my career in his hands – after all, it wasn't looking like it would be much of a career.

Sammy saw something in me that others didn't. I have asked him what it was and he can't give me an answer. He just says he saw a spark.

At the time, Sam was working in a mega-management business called All Sports. Between them they had just about every player in the game.

Sam didn't need to waste his time on a kid who didn't have a deal and didn't ever look like getting one. I will be forever grateful to Sam for taking me on. I have had plenty of managers try to poach me over the years but there is no way I would ever leave Sam. My loyalty is a small repayment for the faith he showed in me early on.

I was stoked to finally have a manager. It wasn't as good as getting a Broncos tracksuit but it was the next best thing.

CHAPTER THIRTEEN

GARY REEN WAS THE coach of the All Whites A-grade team. He approached me with a proposition not long after I turned 17.

'You want to come play in my A-grade team?' he asked. 'I think you're good enough to play against men.'

'Yeah, I'll have a crack,' I said, confident and cocky. 'Sounds good.' And it did, at least until I started training with my new team.

What the hell are you doing? They're going to kill you!

Have a look at the size of them ...

My new teammates were all battle-hardened giants, behemoths with beards and bulging biceps. I looked around the field and saw warriors. There were players who had just come back from grade, including Mick Kennedy, David Anderson and Shane Wilson.

Anderson had only just finished a stint in Sydney with the Parramatta Eels.

Heck. I'm going to get myself killed.

Anderson must have sensed my fear. 'Don't worry, little fella,' he said. 'We'll look after you. Anyone who takes you on will be taking the rest of us on too. We've got your back, son.'

Despite the reassurance, I went straight to the shop the next day.

'Where's the headgear?' I asked.

Being so young, and so small, I wanted to protect myself as much as possible. I wasn't even 70 kilograms yet. So I got myself my very first headgear and I have worn one in every match since. Still, even with the headgear, I was scared stiff.

'You'll be coming off the bench,' Reen said. 'We'll ease you into it. Don't worry about anything. Just get on and do your thing. You won't find it too much different from the 19s.'

We were playing a team called Wattles. They were an outfit brimming with talent, including a local named Tony Duggan. 'Your teammates will look after you,' Reen promised. 'You'll be sweet. Remember, they're all old blokes and they're slow. They can't hurt what they can't catch.'

I sat on the bench, waiting to be thrown into the fray. Behind me were rows of cars up against the fence, blokes inside drinking beers and beeping horns. The atmosphere was next-level.

You got this. It'll be sweet.

My confidence ended up shading my fear. I was never lacking when it came to having faith in my own ability, and while I was scared, I was also excited for the test I would soon face.

'You're on,' Reen said, the call coming in the first half. Chest puffed, head held high, I raced onto the field like I belonged. I demanded the ball straight away and I got it. I tucked the footy under my wing and ran straight into the defensive line.

Whack!

Three grown men smashed me. I hit the ground hard, but sure enough I got up and played the ball.

Not so bad. I can handle this.

That run gave me the confidence I needed to forget about who I was playing against. It was just another game of football: same game, different people. And after a few games I was able to compete comfortably.

The elevation to the adult team saw my game come on in leaps and bounds. I felt like a giant when I went back and played against kids my age. They were just boys. After taking on men who were trying to take my head off, I was back squaring off against kids. It seemed all too easy. Seriously, I ran amok when I went back to the 19s or 17s. It was like stepping back three levels. I felt like I couldn't be stopped.

Moving up to play A-grade was one of the best decisions of my career. I had never been the strongest defender, but taking that step really helped me with my tackling. It gave me the confidence to actually hit and stick when I came back to my own grade. After having 30-year-old rough nuts running at me, the biggest 19-year-old no longer seemed so big.

Playing A-grade also exposed me to better coaching. I was learning things like inside and outside shoulder and the basics of rugby league structure. I wasn't in an NRL system but I no longer felt I was being left behind.

Things were finally looking good. I had made the Queensland Under 17s, I was making a name for myself in A-grade and I had a manager fighting for me behind the scenes. And I was pretty well behaved. I was focused on my footy and I made good on my vow to stay away from stealing and smoking. And I also started growing. While I was still the lightest, I was no longer the shortest. I shot up all of a sudden. Yep. Life was good.

I moved in with Rob Walmsley and his partner Kate Fahey. Rob was one of my coaches. They were great to me and I was comfortable with the little bit of money I was getting from ABSTUDY, a government fund for Indigenous students.

Mum, Dad and Uncle Dean were coming to visit me on weekends, and I was doing OK at school. I went to Toowoomba with hopes of getting an OP (overall position) – the Queensland equivalent of a Higher School Certificate (HSC) – which would have given me a shot at a higher education. But I dropped out after I began Year 11 and took on vocational subjects instead. I found the OP path too difficult while trying to pursue my football dream. To succeed I would have had to study a couple of hours every night and I wanted to spend the time working on my football game instead. It was rugby league or nothing. And it was about then that I suffered a blow that had me thinking I was heading towards the latter.

I sat on the ground, legs crossed, head up, waiting to hear my name. I was covered in dirt, drenched in my own sweat, bloody and bruised. The Queensland Schoolboys Carnival, held in the stinking heat of Cairns, had just finished. I had given it my all.

A Queensland selector walked over, sheet of paper in hand. 'Congratulations on a great carnival, boys,' he said.

'We'll now be selecting the Queensland team to play at the Australian Schoolboys Championships. If your name is read out, please walk over to the table and collect some paperwork. If it's not, then keep your head held high.'

The selector started selecting, names rattled off one by one. I was certain my name would be called. I thought I had been one of the best players in the entire carnival. I waited, waited and waited some more.

'And that's all,' the selector said. 'Better luck to those of you that are coming back next year. To the rest of you, keep at it and all the best for when you leave school.'

What? You missed me?

I thought it was a mistake. It wasn't. I had been overlooked. Again. First I was stunned and then I was shattered. I picked myself off the ground and walked past the parents, the teachers and the NRL scouts. None of them wanted to talk to me. I wandered away from the crowd and cried.

What's wrong with me?

I was so frustrated. I had spent the year playing A-grade and excelled. I had come on in leaps and bounds. And I was sure that I had had a better tournament than most of the guys they had picked.

Turns out they all thought I was too small. They went for kids with bigger bodies, guys like Dane Campbell and Mick Russo. Yeah, they were bigger than me, but not better. And a lot of the NRL recruitment managers decided if I wasn't good enough for the Queensland team then I certainly wasn't good enough for the NRL.

They thought I was too small. And too slow. Again I failed to get a single offer.

I was suffering from a stigma that I couldn't tackle. Everyone would say, 'Oh yeah, he can attack, but he can't defend, he's too small.'

And honestly it was crap. I never missed tackles. It all came down to my size.

So I finished high school without a rugby league club. Despite my two-year turnaround it was the same old story: no one was interested in Johnathan Thurston. I had no NRL deal and no job prospects.

The future didn't look great.

CHAPTER FOURTEEN

BLOOD. GUTS. BITS OF BONE. My apron looked like a crime scene. Freshly washed and white at the start of the day, the garment was now soaking red. I put my mop into a bucket, hot soap slapping against chunks of flesh, and shook my head.

Is this my life now?

Well, at the beginning of 2001, it was. So I picked up my mop and attacked another pile of fat and filth. Time to get back to work. School done and dusted, NRL clubs not interested, my life was now a room full of meat in the back of a supermarket. With nothing but a rugby league résumé and an NRL dream, I took a job as a butcher's assistant when I left school. And I wouldn't even have scored that job if it hadn't been for rugby league.

One of the men I was playing A-grade with, Bobby Cox, was a butcher. When I finished high school he offered me a job.

'Sure,' I said. 'What else am I going to do?'

I took the job. I really appreciated Bobby giving me the opportunity, but it wasn't getting me closer to my dream of playing NRL, so I hated it.

The butchery was located in the back of a Coles supermarket. I was a butcher's assistant and I almost quit after my first day. Wearing heavy overalls covered in blood and muck, I was locked in a freezer for eight hours moving meat – pallet after pallet of beef, chicken and lamb – off the truck and into the shop.

I remember struggling to lift some of the boxes, even though they only weighed 20 kilograms. I was always more speed than strength.

As I worked there cleaning, sweeping and scrubbing until the tiles sparkled white, I wondered where my life was going. I was beginning to doubt I would ever be more than a good A-grade player who moved meat.

My first official knock-back came the year before, in a letter from the Wests Tigers to my management agency. They said they would be watching my progress with 'keen interest' but were 'unable to place' me at their feeder club.

They were the first of many. Soon the Storm and the Roosters would knock me back too.

I decided to put my head down and forget about the setbacks. I was hoping 2001 would bring me some luck. But it wasn't looking good. So I went back to mopping meat ...

Soon I was living solely for the weekend. Monday to Friday became a bore. I was packing boxes and sweeping floors for eight hours a day. The only thing I had to look forward to was football and going out afterwards with my mates. I loved playing A-grade with the boys. But everything else was crap. I was soon struck down by regret.

Why didn't you try at school? What were you thinking? Take a look at yourself now ...

I did and I didn't like what I had become. I was a butcher's assistant who played A-grade on the weekend. The best I could hope for was to get an apprenticeship as a butcher and play football in the park for fun.

I started kicking myself for not doing better at school. I began regretting my decision not to go for an OP and I still do. I really wish I had given Year 11 and 12 a go.

Yeah, I went to school, yeah, I went to class, but I just sat there ignoring it all for the most part. I never gave myself a chance. I should have applied myself to school like I did rugby league. I will never know how well I could have done or what else I could have been.

My rugby league dream was suddenly revived when I made the Queensland Under 19s in 2001. I was selected to play in the curtain-raiser to the State of Origin. Still eligible to play Under 18s and not aligned with an NRL club, I was plucked by the selectors from A-grade to play with and against the best young rugby league players in Australia. I was stunned.

What the hell are they thinking? Is everyone else injured?

I was floating along, living my life. And all of a sudden I was selected to play in the prequel to the last ever game at Lang Park before the famous ground was demolished.

That selection changed my life.

I went into that game determined to have a blinder. I knew I was running out of chances and I felt like it was now or never. I was one of the only guys on the field without an NRL contract. I had to prove that I deserved one.

And I did.

I scored two tries and kicked a bunch of goals in one of my best games. I was a man on a mission and did everything I could to prove the knockers wrong. Having Brent Tate playing outside me helped my cause – he was an absolute weapon. And not even the fact that I scored my second try by running a shepherd could dull my performance.

I took my seat in the stands to watch the main game, knowing I had done all I could. I had no idea what it would do for my career but for the moment I was content to sit back and watch my heroes go to war.

By the end of the match I had forgotten all about my tries and goals, about NRL scouts and contracts. I was back to being a fan as Queensland marched their way to a convincing win over New South Wales. I was on my feet every time they scored a try, clapping and cheering and hugging my mates as Lang Park went wild.

It was in that moment that I decided I had to become an Origin player. It was the greatest thing I had seen in my life. Being in the crowd and witnessing the emotion, well, I wanted to be the one to prompt a celebration like that.

So that is where my real Origin dream was born. I left the ground and went to bed with a big dream. And the next day my phone started ringing ...

CHAPTER FIFTEEN

'JOHNNO!' ROB SHOUTED. 'Quick, come here.' He sounded strangely excited. 'Quick!' he yelled again. 'Someone's on the phone.'

'Righto, coming,' I said.

I waltzed into the kitchen. Rob had the receiver in his hand and a smile on his face.

He shoved the receiver into my palm while nodding with the ferocity of a machine gun.

'Hello,' I said.

'Johnathan?' a man asked.

'Yeah,' I replied.

'This is Nathan Brown,' he said. 'Nathan Brown from the Dragons.'

What the? Nathan Brown? The Dragons player?

I was speechless.

'You there?' he asked. 'Hello?'

'Yeah, mate,' I said. 'I'm here. Sorry, took me a moment to work out whether or not this was a gee up.'

'Na, mate, it's no prank,' he said. 'I just wanted to introduce myself and have a chat with you.'

Now I was smiling ear to ear.

Browny got straight to the point. A former hooker hailing from the NSW North Coast, Brown told me he was doing some recruitment and coaching for the Dragons. He had seen me play the previous night and he had really liked what he'd seen.

'A few people said you're too slow and too small,' he said. 'But every time you ran you made a break in the game. Bottom line is I want you to come to Sydney. How would you like to trial to become a Dragon?'

Wow. Finally I had someone willing to give me an opportunity. Brown wasn't offering me an NRL start, but he said I would play some Jersey Flegg (Under 19s) and the rest would be up to me.

'Ummm,' I said. 'Can I have a think about it? Can you give me a couple of days?'

I wanted to say yes and jump straight on a plane. But first I needed to call my manager, Sam.

'You wouldn't believe who just called me, Sam,' I said.

'Yes, I would,' Sam said. 'Was it Nathan Brown?'

'Yeah, it was,' I replied. 'How did you know?'

'How do you think he got your number?' Sam said. 'Anyway, they aren't the only ones that are interested, JT,' Sam continued. 'I have another club that might be a better option for you. What do you think of the Bulldogs?'

Well, I loved the Bulldogs. I had been a Raiders fan growing up but my dad and my brother supported the Doggies so I knew a lot about them. I had watched plenty of their games at home and they were an awesome club. They had enjoyed huge success since the 1980s and were regarded as one of the most professional clubs in rugby league.

So yeah, I told Sam what I thought of the Bulldogs.

'Good, because they're going to fly you down to Sydney for a look,' Sam said. 'Pack your bag. And I've already spoken to your mum. She wants me to keep an eye on you if you come to Sydney and she's pretty keen on you going to the Bulldogs because I live nearby. There's nothing wrong with the Dragons but the Bulldogs are around the corner from me.'

A week later I was standing in an office at Belmore Sports Ground being offered my very first deal.

'From what we've seen we're prepared to bring you down to Sydney,' said Mark Hughes, the former Bulldogs player turned recruitment manager for the club. 'We're prepared to give you a shot. We'll put you up in a house and get you a job. The rest is up to you. But we want you to come down now.'

Now? Wow.

That wasn't what I was expecting. It was mid-year and I was all settled in Toowoomba. I was expecting them to offer me something for 2002.

'Ummm,' I mumbled. 'Now? I'm not sure. Can't I come at the end of the year?'

I wanted to play for the Bulldogs but I wasn't ready to make the jump. Not then. It was mid-season and I was committed to my A-grade team back in Toowoomba. I didn't think leaving halfway through the season was a good idea. I didn't want to let my team down and I also thought it would be difficult for me to force my way into any of the Bulldogs teams.

But Hughes, whose nephews Glen, Steven and Corey

all played for the Bulldogs, was adamant I join straight away.

'This chance might not be available in six months,' he said. 'But it is now.'

I knew it was the place for me, but I wasn't ready to commit. 'I want to come at the end of the year,' I said. 'I want to finish this season with my team.'

Hughes smiled, knowing he hadn't yet fired off his big gun. 'OK, mate,' he said. 'Well, let's take you to the game tomorrow. You can decide after that. Now let's go and have a look at where you'll live and then we'll go and get a feed.'

I was taken to the 'Belmore house', which is – surprise, surprise – a house in Belmore. Owned by a couple called Pete and Mary, it was where all the young out-of-town Bulldogs lived. Pete and Mary took care of us like we were their own kids. I'll be forever grateful.

I met a few of the residents: future Wallaby Rocky Elsom; Ben Harris, soon to be both a Bulldog and Cowboy; future South Sydney captain Roy Asotasi; and would-be NRL wrecking ball Jason Williams. It all looked pretty good to me.

'What do you think?' Hughes asked.

'All looks sweet to me,' I replied. 'Except for that Williams bloke. He looks like one mean dude. You wouldn't want to end up in a room with him.'

Hughes grinned ...

CHAPTER SIXTEEN

WE HEADED UP THE F3 to Newcastle the next day to watch the Bulldogs take on the Knights in an NRL clash. And in the bowels of Marathon Stadium, Hughes wheeled in his cannon. 'Hi, mate,' said the giant lying on the massage table. 'I'm Steve Price.'

As if I don't know who you are ...

'You got time for a chat?' he asked.

'Yeah, sweet,' I said, completely in awe. 'Here? Now?' He nodded.

Steve Price wasn't just the captain of the Bulldogs. And he wasn't just a Queensland Maroons legend. Pricey was also a Toowoomba boy, and for me that was as good, maybe better, than the other two.

He had my undivided attention.

Between grunts and groans – the massage was rough at times – Pricey told me I had to move down straight away. He told me that coming down at the end of the year would be the worst possible thing for someone like me.

'You won't last, mate,' he said. 'The pre-season will do your head in.'

Pricey told me how people get homesick during the pre-season and that is when most people quit.

'It can be very lonely out there getting flogged,' he said. 'It's much easier if you go straight into playing games. You don't have time to think about how lonely you are.'

It was surreal. Here I was in an NRL dressing room speaking to the captain of the club my father and brother barracked for. Here I was watching the Queensland legend getting a massage.

'Yeah, you're right,' I agreed.

Ha. Who was I to argue?

My mind was made up. I was going to the Bulldogs and I was doing it right away.

I was offered a training trial. I shook hands with Mark Hughes and agreed to become a Bulldog the same day. I wasn't going to get paid a cent so I wasn't a professional footballer yet, but oh man, I was about to feel like one. Did I tell you how much I wanted my own NRL tracksuit?

The contract offered me accommodation in Belmore, plus assistance in finding a job or, failing that, $100 a week through to the end of the season.

So yeah, it was a tracksuit and 100 bucks a week. I had finally hit it big!

Everything I owned fitted into an old cricket bag that I had been using since Year 6. Yep. That was the extent of my life: all my possessions squashed into a Slazenger. I pulled the zipper and put it all on a plane. I was standing in the belly of Belmore Sports Ground a few hours later.

'This is for you, mate,' said the gear steward. He was pointing at a pallet.

'Really?' I asked.

I was staring at more gear than I had ever owned: shirts, jumpers, jackets, pants, shorts, singlets, dress shirts, ties and hats. And it was all Nike.

'Na, that must be for the NRL boys,' I said. 'I'm just here for a trial.'

He shook his head. And with that my wardrobe was tripled.

How good is this?

I had spent my life wanting a Broncos tracksuit but could never get one. So I thought about all the times they had brushed me as I slipped on my very first Bulldogs shirt. I thought about all the knock-backs and what it had taken me to get here. I thought about all the people who told me I was too skinny and that I couldn't tackle.

And then I smiled.

Finally I had my tracksuit, all blue and white and brilliant. And for a skinny bloke it felt pretty snug. I exclusively wore Bulldogs gear from that moment on.

I was sent straight out onto the paddock for a training session with the Bulldogs' Jersey Flegg side after the gear steward kitted me up.

'G'day, mate,' said the Flegg coach. 'I'm Ricky Stuart. You ready to rip?'

Yeah. One of my childhood heroes was now my coach. Of course I was ready to rip.

'Hell, yeah,' I said. 'Let's go.'

Did I mention that part of the reason I wanted to play for the Bulldogs was because Sticky would coach me? I don't think I did. Well, the bloke I used to mimic in the backyard had retired from playing in 2000 and taken up a role as the Bulldogs' Jersey Flegg coach in

2001. It was his first step in what would become a great and long coaching career.

I was starstruck when I walked out to meet Ricky Stuart but that feeling of awe soon passed once I was on the field.

'What is that?' Sticky screamed at one of the boys. 'You're only going half effort.'

I was thrown straight into a fitness drill called a 'four in five'. We had to complete four laps of the football field in five minutes.

'You look stuffed,' he said when I finished. 'But good job. You did it in 4.10. Looks like you're not as unfit as they told me you would be.'

Yep. Sticky just gave me a compliment. Well, I think it was a compliment.

Next came the gym. I had never lifted a weight in my life. Never. And my first gym session at the Bulldogs was one of the most terrifying experiences of my life.

'Full body session, boys,' said veteran Bulldogs trainer Garry Carden. 'Let's rip in.'

I had no idea what he meant. I was put into a group. I watched on as one of the boys bench-pressed 100 kilograms. He pumped out 10, rapid-fire and strain-free.

‘What do you lift?’ he asked.

I looked at the bar and shrugged. ‘Yeah, about that much,’ I said, pointing to whatever he had just thrown around.

Thankfully Carden was within earshot. ‘Start him at 60 kilograms,’ he barked before walking away.

So off came the two 20-kilogram plates. I backed my way onto the bench, a stranger in a strange land. I didn’t even know where to put my hands.

Here goes ...

I pushed at the bar and pulled it off the rack.

It felt like I was holding up a small car.

‘Let’s go,’ Carden shouted again. ‘Push ’em out.’ So I did. One, two ... two and a half.

I couldn’t even get out three. One of the boys grabbed the bar and racked it. I was bright red, partly due to exertion, mostly because of embarrassment.

‘Just the bar next time,’ Carden said.

I looked around expecting to see the boys having a laugh.

But they weren’t.

It was pretty obvious I had some work to do in the gym. All I could do was my best. I had to get stronger.

I looked around and some of the boys were lifting 140 kilograms. I was on the wussy weights, but I was determined to improve.

The Bulldogs' Jersey Flegg side was jam-packed with talent and I had my work cut out to make the side. Some of the best teenage players in Australia were in that team, including Glenn Hall, Roy Asotasi, Ben Harris, Dean Byrne, Brett Oliver, Andrew Emelio and Matt Utai. And they had all been there since the start of the year and done the hard yards. They had earned their start in the side.

And I was the kid from Queensland out to steal someone's spot. Well, that's how it felt. I can't imagine the team's No. 1 playmaker Brett Oliver was glad to meet me. I knew I had to earn the team's respect.

So I went as hard as I could. I nailed myself in the fitness drills. I was a bull at a gate. I was super fit when it came to my cardio and I was determined to show them that I belonged. There was no easing my way in. I had just left my life in Queensland to have a shot at becoming an NRL player. I trained like my life depended on it – because it did.

CHAPTER SEVENTEEN

I MOVED INTO THE Belmore house.

'This is you in here,' I was told, 'And that's Jase, your roomy.'

I looked towards the occupied bed.

Jason Williams was propped against the wall, all 120 kilograms of him being held up by a thin sheet of gyprock. He was covered from head to toe in tattoos. He smiled, flashing his gold-crowned gangsta-style teeth.

'Hey, I'm Jase,' he said in a soft voice before extending his heavily tattooed hand. 'Nice to meet you, bro.'

I wanted to ask him what prison he just left. 'Ummm,' I said. 'Yeah. You too, mate.'

Turns out that Jase was one of the nicest blokes I could ever meet. He was a gentle giant off the field and a killer on it. He will be a lifelong mate, but at first he was just plain scary.

'You're a skinny little dude,' he said. 'We'll have to fix that, hey.'

He soon had me eating raw eggs and downing protein shakes.

'Yuk,' I cried, spitting it back out.

He laughed. 'Na, bro,' he said. 'You'll get used to it. I love this stuff now.'

Jase had an incredible diet – he would eat 10 kilograms of food a day. I would often wake up to find him sitting in bed with a pen and a notepad.

'You studying for an exam, big fella?' I asked.

He laughed. 'Na, JT,' he said. 'Just working out my food for the day. You want me to do a list for you too?'

Why not?

So I gave it a crack. Soon the bloke who drank cans of cola for breakfast and ate whatever was given to him was weighing his food in the morning and placing it in plastic containers.

'I can't eat all this,' I said. 'It all weighs more than me.'

But I did. Bite after bite I ate it all. Soon we were at training – in the Bulldogs gym – and I was sent to the rowing machine for a hardcore pyramid-style drill.

I started feeling sick as soon as I began my first stroke.

This isn't good!

I ignored the rumble in my stomach and kept on pumping away.

Bleeeeewraaahhh!

I spewed all over the floor: raw eggs, cereal, toast and protein shake splattering the rower.

Gaz Carden was soon standing over me. I was curled up on the floor.

'There's a bucket and some rags in the closet,' he said. 'You'll clean up every last bit.'

He walked off laughing, a smile plastered across his face. I think it was his mission to make us spew. Gaz was brutal in the gym. He ended up giving me my very own bucket that stayed next to me at all times.

As for Williams and his diet ... Well, I went and handed him all my food-filled plastic containers when we broke for lunch.

'You get double today, mate,' I said. 'I'm getting a can of Coke.'

When I wasn't training, I worked. My second real job after my stint as a butcher's assistant was at Pickles

Auctions, a company that bought and sold used cars. I was a car washer.

The Bulldogs recruitment manager had the job lined up for me as soon as I arrived. I was to work during the day and train when I finished. I didn't have a car so I used to get up at sunrise and walk to the factory for a 7 am start.

The work wasn't bad and the people I worked with were pretty good too. As I said, it was my job to wash cars. Pickles had a pretty big operation. They had a bunch of machines to speed up the process. I would stand at the end of a giant machine wash. I would wait for a car to come out.

'Let's go!' someone would yell.

And with that, four of us would go mental with rags, rubbing and scrubbing. We would dry down the cars, shine up the wheels, wipe the windscreens, and give the interior a spruce. The used cars looked brand-new once we were done.

I wasn't a football star, so there was no slacking off, turning up late or going home early. I was just like everyone else in that factory.

It was pretty tough rubbing down cars after some of the weightlifting sessions we did in the gym. Some days it hurt just to get out of bed, so wiping down cars could be tough. But I was OK with it all. I was getting paid and I knew I wouldn't be doing it forever.

But I hated being homesick ...

I broke down just three days after moving to Sydney. Ricky Stuart found me hunched over in the tunnel following a field session. Head down, hiding in the shadows, crying.

'You OK, mate?' Sticky said as he put a hand on my shoulder. 'What's up?'

'Oh, nothing,' I said, embarrassed that Stuart had caught me having a cry. 'Yeah. Yeah. I'm sweet.'

Stuart got down on his knees, joining me in the shadows. 'No, you're not,' he said. 'And it's OK. You're not the first bloke I've found like this. Football players aren't as tough as everyone thinks. Come on, mate. You have to tell me what's wrong.'

I wiped away the tears and let it out. 'I feel so alone,' I said. 'I miss my family. This is too hard. I'm not sure I can do this. I don't want to let anyone down but I think it would be best if I went home.'

Stuart put his arm around me. 'Mate, you're homesick,' he said. 'And there's nothing wrong with that. You wouldn't be human if you didn't miss the people you love. The good news is it's not a disease. It will go away.'

I cracked a small smile. 'It will go away?' I said.

Stuart nodded. 'And you're not alone,' he said. 'Take a look around you. You're now part of the Bulldogs family. You have a club full of brothers, fathers and uncles. We're all here for you, mate. I want you to come and talk to me next time you feel alone.'

I picked myself up off the floor and extended my hand. 'Thanks, mate,' I said as I shook his hand. 'I'll be sweet. I'm just a bit of a sook sometimes. I'll be OK.'

And I was OK, for a while. I ripped into the training, went to work, and did my best to get to know the guys in the team. But I wasn't being picked in the team. And I found life tough without football. I walked into Sticky's office four weeks later.

'You know how you said I could always come to you?' I asked. 'Well, here I am. I need to go home. I'm not coping.'

He looked up from the stack of papers he was studying. 'Still homesick?' he asked. 'Or is it something else?'

I shrugged. 'I just don't know if I can do this,' I said. 'I guess I'm homesick.'

Stuart nodded. 'Mate, it's OK to be homesick,' he said. 'Is that all it is? Do you have any other concerns?'

'Well, I wouldn't mind getting on the field,' I said. 'But I understand I have to earn it. I just can't see a light at the end of the tunnel right now.'

Stuart shuffled himself upright, his back leaning hard into his chair.

'You'll get your shot,' he said. 'And you'll get over this homesickness. You're not really thinking about quitting, are you?'

'I'm not sure,' I said.

And I wasn't. I wanted the opportunity and I was grateful for it, but I wasn't getting a start. I didn't want to quit but I certainly wanted to go home and see my family and friends. All the training, working and not playing had taken their toll.

'Look,' he said. 'You have a big future here. You just have to be patient. Why don't you go home for the weekend, see your folks and come back nice and fresh? I'll let you go only if you promise you'll come back.'

I gave him my word.

So I jumped on a plane and headed back to Brisbane. And I had a great weekend with my family and friends. It was so good to see them. I told Mum I didn't want to go back.

'Like hell you're staying here,' she said. 'Johnny, this is everything you've ever wanted. You've worked so hard to get here. You're going to get on that plane and go back and make a name for yourself.'

The weekend was over before I knew it. Mum ordered me a cab.

'Can I stay?' I said, tears in my eyes as I got in the taxi. 'I can try and get a club up here. Maybe they'll want me now that I've been at the Bulldogs.'

She shook her head, gave me a kiss and slammed the door. 'Good luck, son,' she said. 'You show them what you can do.'

I cried the whole way back to the airport.

CHAPTER EIGHTEEN

I WAS BACK IN STICKY'S office two weeks after I returned. There were no tears this time.

'Are your parents free this weekend?' he asked. 'I've got a couple of plane tickets for them to fly down and watch you play.'

That was Sticky's way of telling me I had finally made the team.

'I'm playing?'

He nodded. 'Yes,' he said. 'Well done. I told you you'd get your shot. And that's what you're getting. It's now up to you to make the most if it.'

My parents were free of course. And they were there to watch me have a spew on the sideline before the game.

Bleeeeehhhh!

I emptied the contents of my stomach onto the grass.

'Nerves?' one of the boys asked.

I shook my head. 'Na, I think I ate a bad apple.'

I made my way to the bench. And that is where I waited until I was finally thrown into the game. It was midway through the first half when I ran on. And boy, did it feel good.

Finally. This is what I'm here to do.

I realised how much I loved playing footy and what it meant to me as I ran out onto the field. I looked pretty good in blue and white too.

'Yep,' I called, with outstretched arms. 'I'm here.'

And soon the ball was in my hands and I was stepping my way through a gap. I pinned my head back and went like the wind. The try line was beckoning.

Almost there.

I was about to score a try with my first touch.

Thud!

A desperation tackle from a defender I didn't see stopped me from scoring my first try. I was only inches away from the line. I was so close.

Damn.

Oh well, I might not have scored but making the break gave me the confidence to believe that I belonged on this field with these boys. I knew I was every bit as good as them. And Sticky was pretty impressed with my game. He told me I had exceeded his expectations and that based on that performance I had earned a spot in his side.

About time!

Suddenly all those worries I'd had a couple of weeks before were gone. I was no longer lonely, no longer homesick, and no longer wanting to leave. It is funny what a game of football can do.

I was promoted to the starting side after a couple of more games off the bench. Dean Byrne was promoted to reserve grade so I was thrown into the halves.

And things happened pretty quickly from there.

After another six or so games, I too was called up to play reserve grade. I went from not even getting a start in Jersey Flegg to running out on the field in second grade to play with blokes I had spent my childhood watching on TV.

The Bulldogs reserve-grade team was a ripping side, featuring Steve Reardon, Shane Marteene, Steven Hughes, Reni Maitua and Adam Perry to name a few.

My first match in reserve grade was against Parramatta.

I started on the bench.

'Righto, get on there,' said the trainer. 'You're in for Hughesy.'

Steven Hughes had been injured early in the match and I was chucked into the centres.

I ran out and looked up at the Eels player I was marking: it was future international Willie Tonga.

This is going to be interesting ...

I think I would have been overawed playing my first proper senior match, especially given that I was playing out of position, had it not been for my A-grade experience with Toowoomba. I had played against men before so I just took it as another game.

I went out and did my thing and had a blast. I put my wing partner – Matt Utai – away a couple of times and scored a try myself. I even took over the goalkicking late in the match. It was more than I could have ever expected. I thought I might get a few minutes off the bench at the end, not 77 minutes, a try and a couple of goals to boot. I finished wanting more.

And that is exactly what I got.

A game or two later when we played Cronulla, I was lying on the dressing room floor at Shark Park in tears.

I had just been taken off the field after copping a huge knock to the head. I looked up and Garry Carden was standing over me.

'The only thing he needs is a Gatorade,' Carden said. 'He's crying so much that he is in danger of dehydrating himself. Other than that, he's fine.'

I finished the year playing another three games in reserve grade and became the starting No. 6 in Jersey Flegg. I also became the full-time goalkicker. As I said, it all happened very fast. That homesickness I had felt was but a distant memory.

We went on to win the Jersey Flegg competition, beating the Sharks 12–10 in the grand final. And I played my part by making a gutsy cover tackle to stop a try that would have cost us the match. The jubilation I felt when we won the game far outweighed any of the pain I had previously felt. I was as happy as I could be.

And I have to thank Sticky, not only for being supportive but also for being a great teacher. I really learned a lot from Sticky that year. He was a former half, one of the greatest ever, so I was always picking his brain. I was still predominantly a ball-runner so I wanted to improve all the other areas of my game.

Ricky taught me about game management, something that was utterly foreign to me. I don't think I had even heard the term before I got to the Bulldogs.

Sticky also helped me with my general play kicking. It has always been OK, but a kicking game is always something that can be improved. There is no such thing as a perfect kicking game. I needed to work on finding space. I needed to get the ball away from the wingers and the fullback.

My passing game had always been strong but Sticky helped me improve by working on pass selection. Being a great passer isn't just about being able to fire a football. You need to know when to pass the ball and when to hold it.

As I said, all my doubts were gone as soon as I got on the field. I knew this was the place I wanted to be.

And I finally got to sign my first ever contract on 12 October 2001. It had taken me a long time to get a deal, so I was pretty stoked when I finally got to put pen to paper. I agreed to a one-year contract with a one-year option in my favour. Getting paid to play football was a dream come true. What's better than a tracksuit? A tracksuit and some cash, of course.

I had also expressed interest in starting an apprenticeship and asked the club if they could help, but they decided my maths wasn't strong enough, and neither did I have the 'passion' to commit to a four-year electrician's apprenticeship. Oh well. I had plenty of passion for footy, and I could count by one, two and four, which is the only maths I needed on the field.

After spending six weeks back home – laying bricks for cash and catching up with family and friends for fun – I returned to Belmore. And I was dreading my first ever NRL pre-season.

It can't be as bad as they say. Can it?

CHAPTER NINETEEN

I HAD HEARD HORROR stories about pre-season training. It was all sweat, spew and scorching sun, according to anyone I had ever asked. I was also nervous about joining the NRL boys. I had been selected in an extended NRL squad for the pre-season. I was going to get to train alongside some of the biggest names in rugby league and I was nervous.

So I tiptoed my way down the tunnel hoping for an anonymous entry. I quietly walked into the dressing room and carefully placed my bag on the floor next to a plastic chair. I thought I hadn't been seen.

'Na, mate,' said Brent Sherwin, the Bulldogs NRL halfback. 'Don't put your bag there. You have your own locker now. Come over here. I'll show you.'

I smiled. 'Seriously?' I said. 'Na. Not me. I'm not even a proper reserve-grade player.'

Sherwin laughed. 'Na, you're one of us now,' he said. 'And don't smile. You might not think that's such a good thing when Gaz is finished flogging you.'

At that point I didn't care how tough the pre-season was going be. And nothing could wipe the smile from my face. I had just been accepted into the NRL by way of locker. I was ready for anything.

It was both exciting and daunting to join the NRL squad for the first time. Sure I knew a couple of them from playing reserve grade, but most of the guys were more heroes to me than teammates. I was about to train with Willie Mason, Steve Price, Mark O'Meley (the Ogre) and Braith Anasta to name a few. These guys were Australian Kangaroos and State of Origin players, the best of the best. I felt like a very small fish about to go for a swim with great whites.

I didn't have a lot of time to think about the company I was keeping. Soon the only thing on my mind was pain. We went out onto the field and began our pre-season with a notoriously brutal fitness drill called the 'beep test'. The 'beep test' measures how fit you are by way of survival. You run a prescribed distance and have to make it to the line before hearing a 'beep'. You wait, catching your breath, until another 'beep' starts a fresh run. At first there's a lot of time between the beeps and it is quite easy to get to the line. But the time between the beeps shortens with each run. Eventually it becomes impossible. You keep on going until you fail to make the line before the 'beep'. You are told what level you made it to when you drop out. I think I was in the 12s.

I went as hard as I could and ended up one of the last players standing – well, standing until I collapsed. I was exhausted. And then I was told to get up and go for a run ...

Each day saw a new type of torture: riding, running, lifting, sprinting, pushing and pulling. The only thing that was constant was that we moved until we dropped. The gym work was especially difficult. I had never even trained full time, let alone faced a Bulldogs pre-season, so I found it tough. I couldn't walk at the end of most days and was sound asleep by 7 pm.

I was determined to impress and promised myself I wouldn't be broken. While I didn't think I could earn a spot in the NRL that year, I made it my mission to earn the respect of the team. I didn't want to have another cry in the tunnel. The training broke plenty of players, but I got through my first ever pre-season in one piece. I had my moments, but I made it out the other side. And I was the better for it.

I headed into season 2002 the fittest I had ever been. And I was stronger than I had ever been, heavier too. I ended up putting on three or four kilograms and entered the season weighing 78 kilograms. My body was beginning to change shape. That extra weight and strength gave me an oversized injection of confidence. I set myself the goal of making my NRL debut that year.

My first mission, of course, was to nail down my spot in reserve grade. When I had achieved that I was going to do all I could to get my NRL crack. I got my first taste of the big time when I was taken to Toowoomba for an NRL trial match.

Corey Hughes, the NRL hooker, walked up to me the morning after my very first NRL trial match. He smiled as he threw out his arm.

'Congratulations on your game,' he said. 'You really killed it. Well done.'

I had scored four tries the night before in a dream match played in front of my family and friends. I had come back home and I had nailed it.

'Thanks, mate,' I said as I stuck out my hand to meet his for a shake.

Hughes pulled his arm away and with the speed of a striking snake gave me a smack in the face.

'Ha,' he said. 'Got ya. You got a big head or what?' The entire team laughed as one.

Oh no. What was that?

I went bright red, the butt of the joke and firmly the fool. Oh, I felt terrible. He burned me good. I backed away pretty fast. The boys continued to laugh. Yep. That is how I was welcomed to grade, with a slap in the head and an ego-crushing comment. But hey ... at least they now knew who I was.

The weekend had gone better than I could ever have hoped. I had made the most of my opportunity by putting my name up in lights. And I did it in Toowoomba, the place where I had turned my life around, on a ground where I had played and triumphed with the All Whites.

Jersey covered in dirt, body battered and bruised, I walked to the fence and shook hands with people I knew after the match.

'Hey, deadly,' a little Indigenous fella yelled. I turned, thinking he was talking to me. 'Na, not you,' he said and then pointed at Braith Anasta. 'Him. Yeah, you deadly, Braith. We love you.'

I burst out laughing.

'What?' said Anasta. 'What are you laughing at?' 'That's hilarious,' I said. 'Yeah, you deadly, Braith.'

I continued to laugh. I couldn't stop. And from that day on the boys called me 'Deadly'. No one ever called me JT at the Bulldogs, it was always Deadly. And all the Canterbury boys still call me Deadly to this very day. It wasn't the best nickname but it wasn't the worst. Not when blokes in my team were called Smack (Corey Hughes), Ogre (Mark O'Meley), Nugget (Adam Perry), Shifty (Brent Sherwin) and Pig (Brett Oliver).

CHAPTER TWENTY

I STARTED THE YEAR WELL. I had locked down the No. 6 jersey in reserve grade and was in good form. Both Kevin Moore (the reserve-grade coach) and Steve Folkes (the NRL coach) were happy with my progress.

I was called into Folkes' office after seven games.

Have I done something wrong?

I nervously knocked on his door.

'Come in,' Folkes said. 'Take a seat.'

I sat and sweated on what was about to come next.

'We're going to have to fly your parents down to Sydney this weekend,' Folkes said. 'Have they ever been to Penrith?'

I shook my head. 'I don't think so,' I said. 'Why would they go to Penrith?'

Folkes laughed. 'To watch you play in the NRL,' he

said. 'You want them to be there to watch you make your debut, right?'

And it hit me. I was being picked to play in the NRL. *Woohoo!*

I was so pumped that I couldn't get a word out. All I had ever dreamed of was playing first-grade football and here I was, in front of an NRL coach, being told that my dream was about to come true. It was pure jubilation. A lifelong goal reached.

'Oh, and don't tell anyone other than your parents,' Folkes continued. 'We don't want anyone finding out. You won't be named in the team. We want to keep it a surprise for Penrith. That will also keep the media away from you.'

I nodded, but I wondered how I would go keeping this news quiet. It was the best thing that had ever happened to me. I wanted to tell the world.

I turned up to Belmore the next day as nervous as I was excited. I was a kid on his first day of school. I had done the pre-season with the boys but I hadn't had a lot to do with them since then. And I knew I had to slot right in like I belonged. I didn't want to be stuffing things up at training and getting in the way.

Top left: Barefoot footy at Souths Sunnybank. I didn't own a pair of football boots until I was 10 years old.
Top right: With my younger brother Shane in Sunnybank.

Bottom: First time in Maroon! In 1995 I was a State representative on the footy field. Here I am with the Regional reps from my school.

(ALL PHOTOS THURSTON FAMILY COLLECTION)

In 2001 I finally got a club tracksuit (and a whole bunch of other gear), and boy was I happy. You can see it on my face here, at practice with the Canterbury Bulldogs at Belmore. That's Nigel Vagana whose back you can see – a great bloke, I learned a lot from him.
(Brett Faulkner/Newspix)

First XIII at St Mary's College, Toowoomba in 2000. I'm in the front row centre, and you can see Jaiman Lowe, who I would later play with at the Cowboys, behind me to the right.
(St Mary's College)

And we won! Canterbury Bulldogs defeated Cronulla Sharks 12–10. Nothing in my world to date has felt as good as this moment. (MARK EVANS/NEWSPIX)

Who would've thought it? Aged 21, with Bulldogs captain Steve Price injured, I got a start in the 2004 NRL Grand Final against the Sydney Roosters at Olympic Park, Sydney, 3 October 2004. (BRETT COSTELLO/NEWSPIX)

What a moment. The first of my four Dally M Medals was a complete shock. This is me suited up again, at the ceremony at Sydney Town Hall, 6 September 2005. (GRANT TROUVILLE/NRL PHOTOS)

I'm going to miss these guys. North Queensland Cowboys players and staff, after my final game at Cbus Super Stadium on the Gold Coast, 1 September 2018. (GRANT TROUVILLE/NRL PHOTOS)

Playing for your country is always a great honour. I made my Test debut in 2006, but this photo was taken a few years later, at the Four Nations Final in the UK on 14 November 2009. The Kangaroos thrashed England 16–46, and I was Man of the Match as well as top scorer for the series.
(Matthew Lewis/Getty Images)

Since 2010, the NRL pre-season has includ
an Indigenous All Stars vs NRL All Stars gam
the winning team taking home a trophy na
after the first Indigenous Australian to capta
national team, Arthur Beetson. Here's me w
the trophy in 2015, when the Indigenous A
Stars won 20–6. (Grant Trouville/NRL Phot

Before my final NRL game at Cbus Super Stadium on the Gold Coast, 1 September 2018, with Sam, Lillie, Charlie, Frankie, Dad and Mum. (Chris Hyde/Getty)

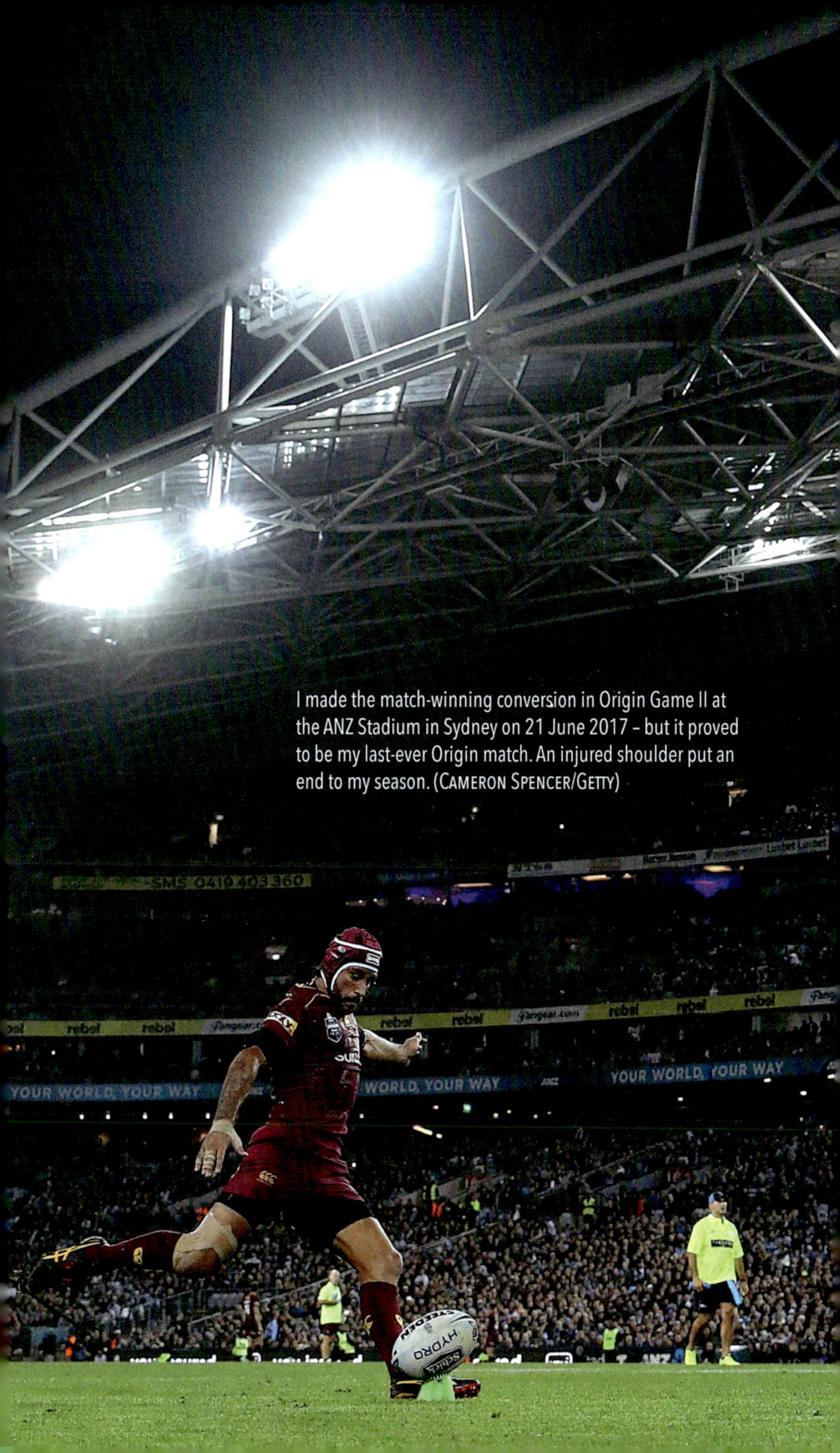

I made the match-winning conversion in Origin Game II at the ANZ Stadium in Sydney on 21 June 2017 – but it proved to be my last-ever Origin match. An injured shoulder put an end to my season. (CAMERON SPENCER/GETTY)

This photo says it all – here I am playing for the North Queensland Cowboys. We beat the Brisbane Broncos 26–20, September 16, 2016. (Grant Trouville/NRL Photos)

'Hey, it's Deadly,' one of the boys shouted. 'You Deadly, JT. Come on. Jump in.'

And with that I felt at home.

'I want you to add some spark,' Folkesy said later. 'Get out there and break the game open.' He told me I was going to come off the bench. His plan was to move Braith into the forwards and put me in at No. 6.

Sweet.

It sounded good to me.

I trained well all week. I knew all the plays because they were the same as the ones we did in reserve grade. The Bulldogs unified their calls across the grades so we could slot right in. The only difference was some of the boys had their own individual calls.

For example, Nigel Vagana – our strike centre – had a call for when he wanted to be hit with an out-ball. Luke Patten (General) had a call for an in-ball. I learned them, committed them to my memory bank and was all set to go by the end of the week.

I sprang out of bed on game day and cracked a huge smile.

Finally.

The wait had been excruciating. I don't think I slept much the night before. I was like a kid on Christmas Eve.

Now what do I do?

It was a night game so I had a whole day to kill. I had never had a game-day routine so I was at a loss. Some guys are religious with their routines. They will do the same thing before every match. Some watch movies, others play golf, some even go out and mow the lawn. I ended up hanging out with Mum and Dad. They had flown in the day before so it was a good opportunity to spend some time with them. They kept my mind off what was ahead.

Soon it was time to go. I put my prized tracksuit on and walked to the Canterbury League Club, where a bus would take us to Penrith Stadium for the clash against the Panthers. I jumped aboard.

'Hey, Deadly,' someone said.

I nodded and smiled before making my way to an empty seat. I planted my bum and settled in for the ride. I don't think I said a word for the duration of the hour-long trip. I just sat back and took it all in. I watched the boys: some played cards, others listened to music and a few just stared out the window, their minds seemingly vacant.

I don't think I thought about the game once. I was just stoked to be on the bus with the NRL team. I was one of them now: an NRL player proper. It would have been pointless to make a mental plan for the match anyway. I was on the bench so I didn't know when I would be on or where I would be playing. I only had to remember one word: spark.

I felt 100 foot tall and bulletproof when I walked off that bus. Dressed in my tracksuit – *yeah, my very own tracksuit* – I was all chest out and head held high as I made my way into Penrith Stadium. We approached a posse of Panthers fans, Willie Mason walking in front of me, Andrew Ryan (Bobcat) behind.

How good is this!

Then came the insults.

Bulldogs suck. Woof! Woof! Dirty dogs. You suck!

Again ... *How good!*

I had never been booed at before.

Yeah, you made it now, Johnny.

Yep. This was the NRL. Boos and all. I couldn't believe I was part of this team. The boys had just won five matches in a row. There was an air of arrogance about them. It was almost as if they thought they couldn't lose. They didn't give a toss about insults. They took every slur as a compliment.

I walked into the dressing room and sat down. Again I just watched; I wanted to take it all in. Some of the boys got massages and others got strapped. Some cracked jokes and others listened to music.

I can't even remember who handed me my first jersey. I was that nervous I don't think I even took notice. I just grabbed it and whacked it on. I do remember looking down at it when I put it on.

This is your first NRL jersey. Sweet. Maybe I'll get it framed.

It was a Saturday night and Penrith Stadium was packed. Soon we were running out onto the field proper. Pre-match speech done, all revved up and ready to go, I sprinted out onto the ground to a deafening roar. Whatever they were shouting was inaudible, just a mess of sound. I was jumping out of my skin, all adrenaline and ready to let rip. And then it was back to the bench.

I took a couple of deep breaths and the frigid night air snapped me back to earth.

Stay calm. You can't waste your energy now. The referee blew his whistle and the game began. *Woah, this is fast.*

This was the closest I had ever been to an NRL match and the speed of the game staggered me. So did the collisions.

Whack!

One of the boys put on a heavy hit and a Panther went crashing into the ground. I wasn't a good spectator. I shook as I watched. I twitched as I waited. And finally I jumped to my feet when I got the call.

'You ready, Deadly?' Bulldogs football manager Garry Hughes asked.

Of course I was.

'You're on.'

And with that I became an NRL player.

CHAPTER TWENTY-ONE

I CHARGED ONTO THE FIELD, taking my place in the defensive line and turned my attention to the opposition. Tony Puletua, a Panthers giant, was staring me down. He gave me a nod before getting the ball. Soon he was steaming at me, his legs tree trunks and his body brick.

Here we go!

Puletua would have been at least 30 kilograms heavier than me and he was coming at me like a steam train. I felt no fear, no hesitation as he charged.

Whack!

I hit him with everything I had, which wasn't much. And he was as hard as nails. The impact threatened to bounce me but I held on with everything I had. Hands still on his body, I slipped down and grabbed at his legs.

And somehow I managed to drag him down. Geez, it felt good.

But I didn't have time to dwell. Before I could think the ball had been played and I was chasing someone else. And that is how it went for the rest of the night. I rushed from play to play, legs pumping, heart racing, always chasing. The speed of the game was staggering.

The biggest difference between the lower grades and the NRL is the speed. Everything in the NRL is just so much faster. There are no stops or breaks. You can't blink. Sometimes you can't even breathe.

'Your ball, Deadly,' said Nigel Vagana, the Kiwi international playing at right centre. 'Go on, have a run.'

A scrum was setting just metres out from our own line. 'Are you kidding?' I said. 'You want me to run it off our own goal-line?' He nodded.

'They'll pick me up and put me in the stands,' I said. 'No way.'

He stared daggers. 'This is your debut,' he said. 'Go and have a carry. Get it out of the way.'

I shook my head and then got as far away from the scrum as I could. Yep, the future Dally M Medal winner dogged it. There was no way my first hit-up in the NRL was going to end in disaster. I would have been picked up and thrown over the dead-ball line.

I remember avoiding my first run but I don't remember making my first run. The rest of the night is a blur, a rush of emotion. All I know is I went OK and we won. I sang the team song in the shed after the match and had a beer on the bus. I met Mum and Dad back at the Canterbury League Club.

'You made it, Johnny,' Mum said. 'I'm so proud.' I could have died there and then.

I kept my spot in grade and a career highlight came in round 21 when I went over for my first NRL try. And believe it or not I scored it in North Queensland against the Cowboys. I ended up getting a double at Dairy Farmers Stadium. No wonder I love that ground.

The Bulldogs welcomed me immediately. I was taken into the fold as soon as I got there and included in their weekend plans. That was part of their culture – you were immediately taken in as family. I felt pretty special being with those boys. Everyone knew who we were. People would stop and point wherever we went.

Some of the boys had huge profiles. Mason, Anasta, O'Meley, they were some of the biggest names in the

NRL. I felt like a rock star although I was barely recognised back then. I had only played a handful of matches and I wore headgear on the field. They would know my name if they asked but mostly they didn't.

I had the most remarkable game of my career a few weeks later. Down 19–0 against the Knights in Newcastle after 40 minutes, we mounted one of the game's biggest ever comebacks to give Hazem El Masri a shot at winning the game. In a thrilling finish, Luke Patten went over in the corner to score a last-minute try and take the score to 21–20. El Masri had a sideline kick on his non-preferred side to make it 16 wins in a row.

He lined up the kick after I bombed a dead-set try, dropping a ball with the try line open earlier in the match. El Masri could erase my mistake with one clean strike. And he nailed it.

Cue the party.

We were on cloud nine after the match, celebrating like we had won a final. We were on top of the world, still undefeated and flying. We had proved to ourselves we could do anything by coming back to win that game. The premiership was ours. We didn't think anyone could stop us.

But we were wrong.

The NRL dropped a bomb. On 23 August Steve Folkes called me into his office. I had gone back to reserve grade the week before, after having a shocker against the Warriors in New Zealand. I was hoping he was about to give me a reprieve.

'Johnno, I've got some bad news,' he said. 'We're about to be stripped of all our points and will spend the rest of the year playing for nothing more than pride. The NRL has just completed an investigation and it looks like we've breached the salary cap.'

I became part of what was labelled one of the biggest scandals in rugby league history when the Bulldogs were stripped of 37 competition points and fined $500,000 for deliberately breaching the salary cap. An NRL investigation revealed the club had exceeded the $3.25 million salary cap by over $1 million for two consecutive years. The stripping of 37 points guaranteed that we would finish with the wooden spoon.

I was stunned.

I walked out of Folkesy's office feeling completely numb.

I couldn't believe what I had just been told. No rugby league team had ever been rubbed out of the competition for a salary-cap breach. I don't think a team had been wiped out for any sort of breach. My confusion soon turned to anger and I stayed angry because no one ever explained why and how this had happened. The only information I got was from reading the papers. It was meant to be such a big year for me. I was playing first grade and on track to be part of a premiership team. And now I would spend the rest of the year playing reserve grade because my NRL match payments would have constituted another salary-cap breach.

I was largely shielded from the drama. I had been dropped back to reserve grade the week before the grenade and I spent my days with Kevin Moore and the second-grade squad. And even when I ended up with the NRL guys, the media were never interested in me. Guys like Braith and Willie were hammered; I was pretty much left alone.

A scandal like this would have broken most clubs – but the Bulldogs weren't most clubs. In the end it was the bond I spoke about earlier that saved the club. Instead of being divided, the Bulldogs became even closer. It became 'us against them'. It was the start of the 'siege mentality' that the club has made famous. We were all watching together when the Roosters won the premiership.

'They're not the real premiers,' one of the boys said. 'They didn't beat us.'

We all vowed to come back bigger and better. We wanted revenge.

CHAPTER TWENTY-TWO

I THOUGHT 2002 COULDN'T get any worse – and then I was picked to play for New South Wales. Yep. This proud Queenslander was told he would be wearing a blue jersey and playing against his beloved Maroons in an Under 19s State of Origin match. Ha. Seriously, I didn't care. Not back then.

I was selected to play in the New South Wales Under 19s team because I now lived in Sydney and played for a club based in New South Wales. I had played for the Maroons the year before when I was based in Queensland. You didn't get to choose who you played for back then – you were told. And I had no problem with turning out for the Blues.

It was a bit strange putting on that jersey and lining up against a bunch of my friends – but I was just happy to be testing myself against the best players in the game.

We went on to win the match with soon-to-be Maroons Willie Tonga scoring three tries and Ashley Graham two.

It was a time of transition for Queensland when it came to State of Origin. They were forced to have a good hard look at their entire football program in 2000 after they were given a 3–0 hiding against New South Wales. Beaten 56–16 in Game III, they had 104 points scored against them in the series. This caused a shake-up from the grassroots level.

In response, Queensland set up the rugby league program at the Queensland Academy of Sport (QAS). They began identifying the best young Queensland players and putting them into camps.

I went into my first QAS camp in 2002. The QAS brought its young Queensland rugby league players together and began introducing them to the Queensland State of Origin system. Since 2001, 51 players have graduated from the QAS to play State of Origin for Queensland. I have no doubt the program paved the way for Queensland to become the powerhouse it is today. Since 2006, Queensland have only been beaten in two series.

After making my debut, and getting a taste of the NRL, it was my plan to establish myself in first grade. I was hoping to earn a starting spot and play in every match that year. But 2003 was not the breakthrough year I was hoping for.

Things didn't work out how I planned. With Braith Anasta and Brent Sherwin performing at No. 6 and No. 7, I had to bide my time. I was resigned to a utility role in 2003, coming off the bench in six of my nine NRL matches.

I tried to make the most of my opportunities, which were limited, and I scored four tries. I worked hard behind the scenes to develop my game. I also ripped into the weights in a bid to put on some size.

The Bulldogs made it all the way to the preliminary final. I thought they would win the competition but they were tossed out by the Roosters in a 28–18 defeat. I was determined to have a huge off-season and break into the squad for season 2004.

I went into the 2004 season with great hopes. I'd worked hard over the pre-season and after our near-miss at a grand final berth the previous year, I was full of confidence. I started negotiating to stay at the Bulldogs at the beginning of the year. A great deal has been made of the contract talks that led me to quit the club, so I will put it all on the table.

The Bulldogs offered a three-year contract, saying I would be their number-one five-eighth for the 2004 season, and become one of their 'marquee' players in the future. I didn't sign the deal they were proposing before the season began; both Sam and I agreed I should play and prove my true worth. But then it all went pear-shaped.

The first major injury of my career came five games into the 2004 season. We were playing against the Sea Eagles at Telstra Stadium in Sydney – we won 28–26, by the way, though I wasn't thinking about that too much at the time.

I was stretchered out of the stadium in a world of hurt after breaking both my fibula and tibia, two bones in my lower leg. Until then I had suffered nothing but sprains, cuts, and heavy hits to the head. And it was all pretty innocuous – well, the cause not the result.

As I had done a thousand times before, I jumped

out of dummy half after spotting a gap. It closed. Three Manly forwards crunched me and my leg got caught in a tangle of arms and bodies. I fell awkwardly, twisting and turning before being thumped into the dirt.

Snap!

First came the noise. Next came the pain. 'Ahhhhh!' I screamed. I crashed to the turf in utter agony.

'I heard it crack,' the referee yelled after blowing his whistle to stop play. 'I heard it crack. Get off him.' He'd heard my bone breaking from 15 metres away. And everyone, even those in the bleachers, heard me scream.

'Ahhhhhhh!' I yelled. 'Ahhhhhhh!'

I knew thousands of people were watching me, both at the ground and at home. Every camera in the stadium was pointing my way.

'Help,' I said. 'My leg.'

I wasn't aware of anything that was going on around me.

The agony was all-consuming.

After what felt like an eternity help arrived.

'What is it?' asked the doctor, flanked by the club trainer and physio. 'What's wrong?'

'My leg,' I replied. 'I'm done. Get me off.'

The doctor looked towards the sideline. 'Stretcher,' he shouted. 'He's no good.'

That was an understatement. I did my best to put on a brave face. I gritted my teeth and held back the pain, the effort turning my screams into uncontrollable sobs. I was soon on an examination table, the doctor and the physiotherapist prodding, poking and pushing.

'Na, it's not my knee,' I screamed. 'It's my leg.' The doctor grabbed my leg and gave it a pull.

'Ahhhh!' I yelled, the pain from the pull feeling like a grenade had just exploded in my leg. 'What the hell was that?'

I looked down and saw bone sticking through skin. 'Yeah, you're right,' the doctor said. 'It's not your knee, it's your leg.'

After painkillers were dulling the hurt, I asked, 'How long am I going to be out for, doc?'

'Months,' he replied. 'Maybe more. We'll have to get some scans to see what else has been damaged. But with the breaks alone, well ... it'll be a while.'

I didn't handle the injury well. I struggled. I didn't know what I was in for because nothing serious had happened to me during my short career. I was also off-contract at the end of the year so that was a serious reason for concern. I was only 20 years old. And my team was caught up in a huge scandal. This injury couldn't have come at a worse time. And it all played on my mind.

'You're looking at spending at least 12 weeks on the sideline,' the doctor said when the scans came back. 'You haven't suffered any soft tissue damage but the breaks themselves will take at least three months to heal. We can't insert plates or screw it back together, so we're looking at a natural healing process. You'll have to let your body fix itself.'

I got so low with my injury that Mum and Dad were forced to come to Sydney.

'I want to go home,' I said. 'I can't deal with this.'

The club let me go home, and I had to promise to return.

Mum gave me a stern talking-to. 'You are going back, aren't you?' she said. 'You have to go back. You're tougher than this, son. You can't throw it all away because you got hurt.'

And she was right. I jumped on a plane and went back to Belmore. Things got better as soon as I was able to train. I once again had purpose and a goal to work towards. Head down bum up, I ripped into my rehabilitation.

CHAPTER TWENTY-THREE

I WAS SELECTED TO PLAY reserve grade once I had recovered. The NRL team was flying and I was told I would have to force my way back into the team. That wasn't the only incentive I had to play well. I was also off-contract at the end of the year and fighting for my future.

My first official offer arrived on 1 July.

'Are you serious?' I said to Sam when he told me about the proposed deal.

'That's huge,' I said. 'And Townsville is a pretty good place, right?' I wanted to stay at the Bulldogs but the Cowboys offer was so good I couldn't refuse.

I cried, knowing I was no longer going to be a Bulldog. When I thought of Mark Hughes, Corey Hughes, Steve Price, Jason Williams, Mark O'Meley,

Willie Mason and all the men that had gone out of their way to make me part of the Bulldogs family – I bawled.

They patted me on the back, shook my hand and wished me all the best. I didn't sleep for a week. I had no idea whether I had just made the best move of my career or the biggest mistake of my life. Anyway, I got back into footy and forced my way back into the NRL.

'You got a passport, JT?' Folkesy asked before the Bulldogs' round 26 clash.

I nodded.

'Good,' he said. 'Because I'm taking you to New Zealand this weekend to play the Warriors.'

I was over the moon. It felt like I had just been told I would be making my debut again. I hadn't played in the NRL since my injury and I didn't think I would until I joined the Cowboys the following year. Suddenly I had a chance to be a part of something special. We ended up flogging the Warriors 54–10 on 5 September, and I played well.

And it wasn't the end of playing with the Bulldogs. Folksey called me up to face the Storm, who we beat 43–18. I set up a couple of tries and scored one too. The boys were slapping me on the back after the game.

'Welcome back, Deadly,' they said. 'How good is this? We're going all the way.'

'Bring on the Panthers,' one of the boys shouted, referring to our opponents for the following week. 'Let's smash 'em.'

And then Folkesy called me into his office and I was dropped from the side. I continued to train with the team. It was so hard to be there knowing I wasn't going to be part of whatever they did. They beat the Panthers 30–14.

But when the grand final rolled around, Folksey was back talking to me. 'You're going to play in an NRL grand final. I'm going to start you off the bench for Pricey.'

'You bet,' I said. 'I can't wait.'

He told me I was not going to be named because they were keeping it under wraps.

It was a big week. Every morning we had fans at training. They would be lined up outside, beeping horns, waving flags and shouting our names. Belmore was literally a sea of blue and white. The local butcher even had Bulldogs-coloured sausages.

But while it was crazy on the streets, it was business as usual once we locked the gates. The boys were confident and professional. They trained hard and well. I never doubted that we would win.

Folkesy gave me my instructions a few days out from the game.

'You'll go in for Braith if things are going well,' he said. 'We'll push him into the forwards and you get on at No. 6 and add some spark.'

He told me to break the game apart. 'If things aren't going so well you might not get on in the first half,' he said. 'But be prepared for anything.'

We were out for revenge. For us this was unfinished business. Nothing was going to stop us. This was our destiny.

It was game day before I knew it. Soon I was sitting on the team bus heading out to the biggest game of my life. We departed Belmore, thousands of fans sending us off to the game in a blue-and-white blitz. We were greeted by just as many when we arrived at Telstra Stadium.

We warmed up inside the stadium, which was surreal because every sound we made was amplified in the quiet. Catching a ball sounded like a thunder crack, the noise hitting concrete before bouncing around the cavernous space. I could hear my heartbeat when all was still. The older boys all had that killer look in their eye: O'Meley, Willie Mason, Braith, Andrew Ryan (Bobcat), they were all on. They flooded the room with confidence and calm.

Before I knew it we were running out onto the field to fireworks, flags and fans. The scene was staggering. I lined up for the national anthem, the eyes of the country watching.

Is this a dream? Is this real?

Here I was, just 21, and playing in an NRL grand final. Wow. To be honest I struggled to take it all in. With a tear in my eye, I scanned the crowd for my family.

I took my place on the bench and became a mere spectator.

And I didn't like it one bit. I wanted to be out there.

'Noooo!' I shouted in the 13th minute and my head went down. Chris Walker had gone over to score the first try of the match. The Roosters were up 6–0 when Craig Fitzgibbon nailed the conversion.

The despair was short-lived.

I jumped out of my seat and fist-pumped the air when Matt Utai crashed over 10 minutes later to bring the score back to 6–4. And I clapped when Hazem El Masri made up for missing the conversion by booting a penalty goal to make it 6–6.

We were down by just one point when I came onto the field in the 46th minute after Matt Utai scored and Hazem converted to make it 13–12. I took on Adrian Morley with my first touch, a show and go. Unfortunately he didn't fall for it. He smashed me. I had a hard time staying composed. Everything felt so rushed and frantic. Everyone seemed panicked. But we soon hit the front when Hazem bounced his way over to score a famous grand final try in the 53rd minute.

'They're going to come back at us,' Bobcat screamed. 'But we can't be beaten now. Not if we give it all we have. This is ours if you all put in 100 per cent. This is it. This is the moment we've been waiting for. Let's do it.'

The next 27 minutes felt like an eternity. The Roosters wouldn't go away; wave after wave of red, white and blue came crashing into our defensive line. It was relentless. We held them out. Repelled each and every charge. And then in the dying moments we cracked. I looked up and Mick Crocker made a bust.

I thought we were done. And then Bobcat came from nowhere and brought him down with an ankle tap.

Finally the hooter went and the war was over. We had done it, winning 16–13. I ran at the closest bloke wearing a blue-and-white jersey and jumped on him.

'We're the premiers!' I screamed. 'We did it.'

From there it was a blur of blue and white, bodies everywhere. We jumped up and down, slapped each other on the back and screamed at the moon. The presentation followed and I was given a premiership ring. I went to put it on but couldn't. I looked over towards Pricey. I walked over and handed it to him. 'This is yours mate,' I said. 'You are the captain of this club and I wouldn't be standing here without you.'

He cried as he took the ring and thanked me by giving me a hug. Folkesy ended up giving me his ring in the sheds but I was able to give it back when the club commissioned the jeweller to make an 18th ring. And I wore it with pride.

After the grand final I had a quiet moment to myself.

Wow. You're only 21 and you've won a premiership. Can it get any better than this?

Well, it did ...

CHAPTER TWENTY-FOUR

THE SEASON ENDED WITH a proposition that would make me think about who I was and where I had come from.

'Mate, do you want to play for the Kiwis?' Daryl Halligan asked. 'They want you for this year's Tri-Nations series. You are a Kiwi, right?'

I had to stop and think.

'Well, yeah,' I said. 'Sort of. Technically yes.'

Halligan, a Kiwi legend who was a kicking coach at the Bulldogs, fronted me not long after the grand final. New Zealand coach Daniel Anderson had sent him to make me an offer.

'Do you want to be an international?' he said. 'You can be if you declare your allegiance to New Zealand.'

You would think I would have told him where to go right there and then. 'No, I'm an Australian,' I should have said. 'I'm a Queenslander. I bleed Maroon.'

But I didn't. 'Let me think about it,' I said. 'I'll get back to you.' I wanted to speak to my dad: the bloke who gave me the Kiwi blood. He sat me down and told it to me straight.

'Much as I'd love to see you play for the Kiwis, I don't think you should,' Dad said. 'It would be a huge honour for me and my family, but that's not who you are. You were born in Australia, raised in Brisbane and you grew up supporting the Maroons and the Kangaroos. Knock them back, son. You need to follow your heart.'

Phew!

I called up Daryl Halligan and for the first time in my life, I declared what I was.

'I'm an Australian, mate,' I said. 'I might have some Kiwi blood but I'm 100 per cent Aussie. While it's tempting for what it could do for my footy, I just can't pretend I'm something I'm not. Sorry.'

So with that I turned my thoughts to becoming a Cowboy.

* * *

I thought I'd made the biggest mistake of my life when I touched down in Townsville.

'Are you serious?' I said to Sam as the aeroplane door opened. 'We're going to melt.'

I had just been smacked in the face by a wall of heat, all humid and hideous. The flick of a latch had turned the cool air-conditioned cabin into a furnace.

My manager laughed. 'You're still on the plane, you big girl,' Ayoub said. 'Wait until we hit the tarmac.'

I looked out the door and could hardly see the ground through the metre-high heat haze.

'Na, I think I'll stay here,' I said. 'This plane will eventually go back to Sydney, right?'

He laughed and pushed me into the terminal. 'You'll get used to it,' he said. 'And everything up here is air-conditioned.'

'What, even the football fields?' I asked.

Soon we were walking the streets of Townsville. For a moment I thought it was raining.

'Look, I'm dripping,' I said to Sam. 'I'm leaking all over the footpath.'

He laughed, before noticing he was making a puddle too. 'Yeah, you're right,' he said. 'This is hot.'

We were both soaked.

'You won't be complaining about the Townsville weather in winter,' he said. 'But I'll let you complain now.'

Things didn't get any cooler when I rocked up to my first pre-season with the Cowboys.

Walking into the gym, I said, 'Geez, it's hot in here. Is the AC broken?'

One of the boys shook his head. 'Yeah, it's been broken ever since Billy Johnstone got here,' he said of the infamously tough trainer who was the head conditioner at the Cowboys. 'He broke them all on his first day.'

Turns out Johnstone didn't break them. He just threw them all out. Apparently it used to be like an igloo in the gym: all state-of-the-art climate control and precision comfort. He didn't want his players to be soft so he made it hot as hell.

Johnstone also had the televisions and any other things that made the gym comfortable removed. And that included the fans. He turned it into a sauna. Seriously, it was disgusting. Imagine 30 blokes working out in a 40-degree room in 80 per cent humidity. Oh well.

I wasn't going to let a bit of sweat stop me. I was going to rip in and become the best footballer I could be.

No one at the Cowboys put any pressure on me after I signed my deal – but I put plenty on myself. While they said there was a starting spot for me, I knew I had to work extremely hard to lock it down.

And being the new kid in town I felt I had to prove myself from the get-go. My strength had always been my fitness, so I wanted to nail the pre-season and make an immediate impression. I started a couple of weeks earlier than most of the squad and I got stuck straight in. I set myself a goal of proving myself to be one of the fittest at the club.

Billy Johnstone was ruthless. Every NRL player has heard stories about the Cowboys' trainer – but nothing can prepare you for his fitness regime. A premiership-winning player with the Bulldogs in 1985, Billy is old-school with a capital 'O' and 'S'. Aside from being part of one of the great Canterbury teams, Billy was also a former professional boxer. A local footy legend in the Brisbane competition before moving to Sydney to play with the Bulldogs and then the Dragons, Billy had 27 professional fights.

There is no one like Billy Johnstone. He tried to break me. I knew that was his mission the moment I met him. Only the strong survive with Billy. He weeds out anyone who is mentally weak.

It took me a while to get used to his style of training. But eventually pre-season was over and we could get out onto the field.

CHAPTER TWENTY-FIVE

FOOTBALL IN HAND, I STARTED making magic with a little bloke called Matt Bowen, who we called Mango. While he might have been slack when it came to anything involving fitness, Mango was a freak as soon as a football appeared. He hated conditioning, but come game-specific training time he was next-level. Mango moved across the ground so easily. He was graceful. And boy, he was quick. No one got near him in a 40-metre sprint. His acceleration off the mark was staggering.

I first witnessed Mango's speed back when I was in Year 11 during a high school footy match. Mango was in Year 12 and he had already been making a name for himself. We went to a carnival at Bundaberg and everyone was talking about him.

'You seen this Bowen play?' everyone would ask. 'He's the next big thing.'

I wasn't convinced until I took him on – and lost. We eventually came up against Mango's side and early into the match he made a break. He wasn't completely through and he was right up against the sideline. I had a bit of a start on him and only had to move a couple of metres to shut him down. And that is when he put his foot down and took off.

Damn! He's quick.

He left me clutching at air.

Geez. Wouldn't mind playing with that bloke one day.

And in 2005 I got my chance.

We formed a bond as soon as I arrived. We had a footballing sixth sense in that we just knew what the other one was going to do. I knew where he would be and he knew where I would put the footy. It was a dream combination from day one. I knew from the moment I started throwing footballs to him that I was going to have a good year. I just had to give him a little space and he'd do the rest.

I began the year training at No. 6 and was selected as the starting five-eighth for our first trial match. I was playing second receiver, and the majority of the plays were being run off me. I picked the plays up quickly and became comfortable being the main ball distributer for the team. A lot of that was thanks to our coach Graham Murray (Muzz).

Muzz was a tactician who never left a stone unturned. He was a real student of rugby league, and put a great deal of thought into every play on the football field. He had a great football brain, as did Neil Henry, who was the assistant coach when I became a Cowboy. Together they made a great coaching team.

Muzz was also a good communicator. We were always kept well informed of his plans. We had a couple of meetings each week and constant chats on the football field. Muzz was also big on video. He would put tapes on and show us what we got right and where we went wrong. He did a lot of research on rival teams and came up with specific game plans to attack the weaknesses of our rivals.

This level of preparation was new to me. Sure we did a bit at the Bulldogs, but it was always about us and not them. Both Muzz and Neil were also big on individual preparation. I got a spray off Neil early on.

'What, you think standing around cracking jokes instead of stretching will make you a better football player?' he shouted. 'Well tell me, how many NRL games did you play last year?'

I looked at him like the goof I was. 'Six,' I said.

'Exactly,' he shouted. 'And it would have been a whole lot more if you took your training seriously. You need to act like a professional in all areas of your game.'

I laughed it off but it hit hard at the same time. I never stretched and never took my prehab or rehab seriously. And I knew I would have been back on the field a lot faster the year before if I was a little bit more professional. I think that's when I started treating every area of my training seriously.

My NRL debut for the Cowboys came in round 1 when we played the Brisbane Broncos at Suncorp in Brisbane. I didn't quite understand the rivalry back then. To me it was just another game. But soon I would learn about all the history between the two teams and what beating Brisbane meant to our fans and our club.

North Queensland were very much the Broncos' little brother. And we had grown up in the shadow of the powerful Brisbane outfit. They had it all: cash, glamour and stars. We had pain, suffering and a long history of losing. But as a club we always stood up against the Broncos. No matter how high the odds were stacked against us, we gave them a game. It was this history that helped define the fighting culture of our club.

But for me the rivalry was just a story until I ran out onto the field. I was confronted by deafening noise as I left the tunnel. The ground was packed with screaming fans. I had never seen a crowd as big for a regular NRL match.

And they weren't just Broncos fans.

I looked around and saw Cowboys fans everywhere. There was as much blue, white and yellow as there was maroon and yellow. Thousands of fans had made the 1400-kilometre trip down to Brisbane to watch us play, many of them piling into the car for a 15-hour drive. And that is when the rivalry became real.

My debut wasn't real memorable. We lost 29–16 and were never in the match. Believe it or not, the highlight of the night for me was getting belted.

Whack!

I was looking back on my inside for a runner when I was hit hard, all shoulder and bone.

Who was that?

I went crashing into the ground, falling in a heap. I was cursing myself for taking the wrong option. And then I saw who tackled me.

That was Darren Lockyer. Wow.

I was completely starstruck.

You just got tackled by Locky. By Darren Lockyer. How good is that?

Yep. Lockyer was a hero to me. Still is. And I didn't mind the fact that he had just hammered me.

CHAPTER TWENTY-SIX

I DIDN'T HAVE TO WAIT long to face my former team, with my first clash against the Bulldogs coming in round 2. I was a little nervous about facing my mates – but also keen to get it out of the way. I was expecting them to give me a bit of grief out on the field, but I can't remember anyone saying a word. I don't remember too much about the game – but I do remember getting the win. We ended up beating the Bulldogs 24–12 in front of a near capacity crowd at Dairy Farmers Stadium.

And in round 3, I became an NRL halfback for the very first time in my career. An injury before the Warriors game forced a reshuffle and I was given the No. 7 jersey. I was a little bit unsure of making the move because I had spent the entire off-season as a No. 6 in a distribution role, and I didn't know how I would go with the added responsibility of getting the boys around the park. I was still very much on a learning curve. And now I was learning all the calls and getting the boys to their plays. It was new for me and certainly a big challenge. I looked at it as a way of earning their respect.

We went on to win five of our next six games and suddenly I was being touted as a contender to partner Darren Lockyer in the Queensland State of Origin team. Queensland were looking for a No. 7 to partner Locky in that year's State of Origin series. And my move into the halves to cover for an injury had put me in contention.

I didn't believe it at first. I had a laugh when I picked up a newspaper that claimed I would replace Tigers playmaker Scott Prince as the Queensland No. 7.

Ha. No way. Where do they come up with this rubbish?

I thought it was fantasy.

I started getting cornered by reporters after games.

'Are you up to it? Are you the man to lead Queensland? Can you be the next great Queensland playmaker?'

I would just roll off the stock-standard answers. 'Oh yeah, I think I'm ready but it's out of my hands. I'm just here to do my best for the Cowboys.'

I kept on thinking back to the night I saw Darren Lockyer lead Queensland to victory over New South Wales after I played in the Under 19s State of Origin match. I had been dreaming of playing alongside him ever since that magical moment.

The Queensland selector called early on a Sunday morning. 'We're picking you to play Origin, mate.'

I looked around my apartment, expecting to see one of my mates on a mobile phone. I had brought a bunch of my friends up that weekend and I was sure one of them was playing a prank.

'Na, who is this really?' I said.

'Pack your bags,' said the selector. 'You're going into Origin camp.'

I hung up the phone and jumped up and down on the spot. 'I made the Maroons,' I screamed. 'I'm playing Origin!'

Another six Cowboys made the team and we all travelled down to Brisbane to join the rest of the squad. I was shaking with excitement the entire flight. I had only ever met Darren Lockyer once, and that was when he smashed me on the football field.

* * *

I walked out onto the sun-drenched field.

Is this for real? Look at what you're wearing!

My torso, still all lean, made the size small Queensland Maroons singlet look huge.

'That's the smallest one we have,' said the bloke who handed me my kit an hour or so before.

I didn't care. I grabbed it and slapped it on.

Maroons! You're wearing a Queensland Maroons singlet.

And then there were the shorts. Yep. They were maroon too. All XXXX and QRL.

Wow. This is for real. I'm a Maroon.

I looked towards the field: players passing balls, stepping between cones and stretching.

I felt like a fraud. Like a kid who had gone to Rebel Sports and bought the training kit. I was wearing the gear of the gods. And then I heard my name.

'JT,' coach Michael Hagan said, 'come on. Let's start.'

And with that I became a Maroon. Well, kind of. I was pretty much a passenger for that entire first session.

I was there, standing in at first receiver, shuffling balls, pointing and chasing the play – but I felt I was just watching.

I was in awe of the skill that was on display. Seriously. Mind blown. Everything was smooth, crisp and fast. Every pass hit the mark. Backs exploded, their runs perfectly timed; there were options aplenty for anyone who had the ball. The forwards charged: left, right and straight – every play of the ball faster than the last.

Lockyer was firing bullets. Smithy was hitting nothing but chest. And Petero Civoniceva was knocking defenders flat. It was a level of skill and intensity I never thought possible.

And then Darren Lockyer stopped the session.

'JT,' he said, 'come over here.' He ushered the rest of the team away and I was standing there alone with my hero. 'What are you doing, mate?' he asked. 'Wake up. For me to be able to do my job I need you to do your job. And right now, you're not doing it. You're just catching and passing. I need you to lead the team.'

I nodded. He was right. I was scared stiff of doing anything other than shuffling the ball down the line. I didn't want to overcall Darren Lockyer. I didn't want to jump out and have a run and leave him standing behind, hands on hips.

'You're in the team because I believe in you,' he continued, 'and because I know you can do your job. I need you to take control of the team and get them around the park. That's why the selectors picked you and why I wanted you. I can't play my game unless you take care of yours.'

He must have got a pretty good read on me straight up. He knew how nervous I was and knew that he had to address the situation right there and then. And he was right. I was being tentative with everything I did.

You heard the man. Let's play some footy.

I was a different person as soon as we had that conversation. I admired him and looked up to him. I wasn't going to ignore him.

'Right!' I yelled. 'Two to the left, one to the right, and then my ball.'

I'm glad he pulled me up. It would have been a very different week if he hadn't.

And to know that Locky, a god at the time, was part of my selection in the team made me feel invincible. I walked away full of confidence and self-belief.

CHAPTER TWENTY-SEVEN

THE BUS RIDE FROM the hotel to the match was full-on. I thought I would be prepared after the grand final the year before, but this was next-level. Chris Close (Choppy), the manager, got up before we jumped on and gave the Queensland spiel. He told us what it was all about and got us in the mood.

The atmosphere literally had weight. The game was in Brisbane and the entire city had stopped. It was like the only thing on in the world was Origin, and I was part of the main event.

We had some time off the day before the match and I went shopping in Brisbane with a few of the lads – it was a mistake. For the first time in my life I was a celebrity. I couldn't walk 10 metres without someone pointing, nodding or yelling my name. I was quite embarrassed, to be honest. I didn't really like the attention.

The streets of Brisbane were nothing compared to the ground they call 'the cauldron': Suncorp Stadium. Wow. The noise was out of this world. The ground was at capacity, fans hanging from the rafters. And they were all there for us. I couldn't see a speck of blue in the stands. It was all Maroon.

The first 40 flew. Literally. My first memory of the game is walking off the field at half-time when we were leading 19–0.

Seriously, after my first 40 minutes with Queensland I didn't think State of Origin was what it was cracked up to be. It seemed pretty easy to me. But 25 minutes later I was a mess. Tackling, running, passing and screaming. I was going play to play, sometimes forgetting to take a breath.

I had to look at the scoreboard to make sure it was real. Yep, we were losing by a point. It was 20–19.

New South Wales had come from nowhere to steal the lead. They had scored four consecutive tries, leaving us stunned.

Down by one point and with the siren about to sound, I found myself holding the ball and staring down the barrel of a make-or-break kick. Locky had been going to take a match-saving shot at a field goal the play before but got tackled. So here I was, the very next play, with a chance to level the match.

Or a chance to blow it ...

I didn't have a lot of time to think about it. Ball in hand, all I could see was a blitz of blue coming my way. So I dropped the ball and took a snap.

The field-goal attempt didn't feel good off my foot and Andrew Ryan got a hand to the ball before it cleared the NSW defensive line.

Despite the touch, the ball continued to climb.

It scraped over the posts and the referee blew his whistle. I clapped five times before moving back into position. It was my first ever big-match clutch play, but I didn't have time to celebrate.

With the game all tied up at 20–20, we were going to golden point. Soon we were defending and under the pump. The Blues were attacking my edge and I watched on as Brett Kimmorley threw an all-or-nothing long ball out towards Matt Cooper. The ball went sailing past my face and seemed certain to put the NSW centre into a hole.

Enter Mango.

In one of those freakish football moments, Mango exploded out of our defensive line and attacked the ball. Hands out, feet pumping, he was either going to win us the game by taking an intercept or lose it by opening a hole for Cooper.

He won us the game.

Paul Bowman and Smithy crash tackled Mango to the ground after he went over to score the match-winning try.

Unfortunately, the rest of the series didn't go our way. I was initially pumped when Andrew Johns was selected to make his comeback match after injury for New South Wales heading into Game II.

I had watched Joey play all my life and he was one of my favourite players. It was both he and Locky that I tried to base my game on. Joey, like Lockyer, had been at the top of his game for more than a decade. He could win a match in the blink of an eye.

So I was stoked. I was going to be his opposite number. And I was going to give him a run for his money. Or so I thought ...

Joey gave me a fair hiding in those two games. The closest I got to him was when I was chasing him from behind after he split the line.

Joey laid on tries, made breaks and kicked goals, but he did a hell of a lot more than that. When he came out in Game II, New South Wales was a completely different side. Chalk and cheese. He transformed them from a team that had 19 points laid on them in the first 40 of Game I into a team that didn't entertain the thought of a loss.

Joey was a master, and it was a privilege to be on the field with him when he delivered a masterclass. He is rightfully regarded as one of the game's greatest ever players.

It was not a nice way to end the series after the Game I triumph, but I left the Origin arena with a new-found confidence.

I went back to the NRL and felt like I was a brand-new player. I wanted to dominate instead of just compete. I felt so much more confident competing at the NRL level after being exposed to the greats of the game. It was a similar feeling to when I went back to the 19s after playing A-grade. The Origin arena made me a far better player – and I desperately wanted to play for Queensland again.

CHAPTER TWENTY-EIGHT

I WORE A RENTED SUIT and a nervous smile to the Dally M Awards ceremony later that year. Origin over, NRL finals set to start, I turned up to rugby league's night of nights expecting an ordinary evening. Turns out it was extraordinary.

A camera and microphone were shoved into my face as soon as I arrived. 'We are here with Johnathan Thurston,' former NRL player turned reporter for the night Matt Adamson said. 'You have had a tremendous year and are in the running for the Dally M. How do you feel?'

Tremendous year? In the running? Ummm ...

'A bit nervous,' I said.

That was an understatement. Suddenly I was sweating and shaking.

The Dally M is considered the greatest individual award in rugby league. Following each and every NRL game, an expert judge awards the best player, at least in his or her opinion, three points. The next best gets two, and the third best, one.

I was in second place on the Dally M leaderboard when voting went behind closed doors after round 16. I thought I was playing well but most of the points I was given could be attributed to the fact that I had played halfback and five-eighth in a team that was going very well.

There were 10 rounds of voting to be revealed at the sit-down dinner ceremony. I thought Andrew Johns was about to win his fourth Dally M. He had missed the first half of the year with injury but returned to the NRL and he'd been at his devastating best.

We were all sitting at fancy tables – I was sitting in between my partner and my coach, Graham Murray. 'Let's take a look at the leaderboard after 16 rounds,' said the MC, Warren Smith, after the welcoming speeches.

The top 10 players were revealed; I was coming second with 19 votes – one point behind leader Ben Kennedy.

'Let's take a look at what happened in round 17

before we see which of the top 10 players polled votes,' Smith continued.

A highlights package featuring snippets from all the round 17 games was played on a big screen. I didn't feature in any of the footage.

'Only one player in the top 10 polled,' Smith said. 'Scott Prince: One vote.'

Then it was on to round 18. 'Andrew Johns,' Smith said. 'One vote. Johns moves into the top 10.

'Stacey Jones,' Smith continued. 'Two votes. Scott Prince: Two votes. And Ben Kennedy: two votes.'

But then I started polling votes: one in round 19 and two in round 20. And I stole the lead from Ben Kennedy in round 21, when I was awarded three votes for a man-of-the-match performance in a 26–24 win over Manly.

I was sweating.

Joey was coming. He was trailing by just six points after also scoring three points in round 21.

The gap closed to four points when the votes for round 22 were revealed.

I was neck and neck with Andrew Johns – who would become a rugby league immortal – heading into the final two rounds, me with 26 votes and Joey with 25.

‘Only two players can now win the award,’ Smith said after Ben Kennedy and Scott Prince fell out of contention. ‘Let’s see if either of them polled votes.’

The room was silent as he paused.

‘Andrew Johns,’ Smith resumed. ‘Three points.’

The room erupted in gasps, cheers and applause as the Newcastle legend stole the lead.

‘Johnathan Thurston,’ Smith said, his booming voice silencing the crowd. ‘Three points. Ladies and gentlemen, this is going to go down to the wire. Let’s get to round 26 and find out if it will be Johnathan Thurston or Andrew Johns who takes home rugby league’s greatest individual prize.’

My white button-up shirt, also rented, was now soaked through.

‘Andrew Johns,’ Smith said. ‘Three points.’

My heart sank to my stomach as the crowd erupted once again. We had scraped past the Storm in the final round – 30–24 at Dairy Farmers – and I didn’t think I had played that well.

And then Smith spoke. ‘With three votes against the Storm and winner of the 2005 Dally M …’ Smith said, ‘Johnathan Thurston.’

What? How? What?

It took me a moment to process what I had heard.

You won! YOU WON!

I jumped to my feet, my legs no longer shaking, and kissed my partner. I shook our CEO Peter Parr's hand and then embraced Muzz.

All I could think was 'don't mess this up'. It was the most nerve-racking moment of my career. Seriously. It was more daunting than lining up that sideline conversion at the 2015 grand final. Somehow I made it up onto the stage.

The Prime Minister of Australia, John Howard, draped the medal around my neck.

I took a deep breath.

'Johnathan Thurston,' Smith said. 'The first North Queensland Cowboy to win the Dally M. What a moment and what a finish!'

He looked towards me. 'Step up here to the front of the stage because it is where you belong,' Smith said. 'I can't believe that finish. You just kept on leap-frogging each other. Wow, you are shaking. That was quite something.'

'Yes, ah ...' I said, my voice cracked, my words not quite making it out. 'I'm shocked. Johnsy? He missed out so many games and was still there. But like I said ...' My words failed me.

'You have a rest,' Smith said, saving me. 'What will this mean to Debbie and Graeme, your mum and dad watching on at home tonight?'

'My parents ...' I replied before taking a pause. 'I love them so much. They would be as proud as punch. I'll say a quick hello to them. I love yas.'

I woke up the next morning and people were calling me the best player in the game. In one night I had gone from just a player of the future to an NRL star. The day before, I was doing my best – and now I was the best. Or at least that's what they said. It was a lot to comprehend.

CHAPTER TWENTY-NINE

THE COWBOYS GOT THROUGH to the grand final in 2005, ultimately losing to the Wests Tigers 30–16. The final score was not a true indication of the match. It was a game that we could have won. Should have won.

And I was shattered afterwards. I sobbed on the field like a baby. I had never felt pain or hurt like it. There is a famous expression in sport: 'There is always next year', but right then it felt like there wasn't going to be a tomorrow.

But I picked myself up and I began my 2006 pre-season like a bull at a gate. All effort, burn and nothing left in the tank, I trained like I had never trained before. I went to bed each night exhausted. I woke up sore. When times got tough, I used the grand final loss as motivation.

'Get up,' I would tell myself when I struggled to rise. 'Do you want to feel like that again? Go harder. You need to put in more.'

And each day I did. By the time the season started I was fitter, stronger and tougher.

I ran out onto Suncorp Stadium for our round 1 clash against the Broncos and in a dream start to the season, I scored three tries and kicked six goals in a 36–4 flogging of big brother Brisbane. On their turf, in front of their crowd – all 46,227 of them – I bagged a personal haul of 24 points to help bury the Broncos and bust the second-year syndrome.

And that was just the beginning of a blitz. We travelled back home to beat the Sea Eagles by four points in front of almost 24,000. It was the biggest home crowd I had played in front of since moving to North Queensland. Next up was the Storm – our finals opponents from the year before. I scored two tries and kicked eight from eight as we belted them 40–8. We then proved that kicking 2005 minor premiers the Eels out of the finals was no fluke, by beating them by eight points in our fourth straight win of the year.

And then came the one we had been waiting for.

It had been 187 days since the most heartbreaking day of my life. I ran out onto Dairy Farmers Stadium to face the Tigers for the first time since the grand final loss. I took the field, 20,262 Cowboys fans cheering, just fire and flame. I had one word in mind as I took to the middle: *Revenge.*

And that is what we got when we destroyed the premiers 32–12 in the grand final rematch.

Next up were the Knights. In other words, Andrew Johns. And I was champing at the bit to play against the legend called Joey in our first clash since I shaded him for the Dally M.

While we were undefeated so far that season, the Knights were arguably the form team of the competition. They had won four from five, including a 70–32 win over the Raiders, and were sitting just two points behind us on the table. They were coming into the top-of-the-table clash fresh from flogging hotshots the Dragons 54–6, to rack up a staggering 217 points in just five matches.

There was a lot of talk in the lead-up to the match about the rivalry between me and Joey, and it messed with my head. But once on the field, I was focused.

It's training and talent. It's also skill, strength and stamina. Kicking tee sent flying, ball in the air, the only thing you're thinking about is getting down the other end of the field as fast as you can, in the hope that it's you who makes that first tackle.

And in a down-to-the-wire match, we continued our undefeated season start by beating Newcastle 18–16. While all the talk was about me and Andrew Johns heading into the match, it was Mango who won us the game. The man who sent me over the line to score the try that kept us in the game with a two-pass was Mango, who chipped and chased on the last to put us in front. He then won the match by stripping the ball from Clint Newton after running him down to prevent what seemed a certain try.

I was so glad to get that one out of the way. I ran to Mango and gave him a hug. 'You're the man,' I said.

I was a little bit disappointed that I hadn't made the Tri-Nations tour of the UK at the end of the 2005 season and I had no great hopes of being picked for the Anzac Test, which was to be played on 5 May at Lang Park, given that it was just a squad of 18. Andrew Johns was going to be the halfback and Darren Lockyer the five-eighth.

And then the phone rang.

'You fit and healthy?' said Australia coach Ricky Stuart.

'Mmm, yeah,' I said. 'Why?'

'Because you're going to be playing for the Kangaroos,' he replied. 'I'm picking you on the bench.'

I was completely shocked. Utterly elated. But equally stunned.

The bench? Me? Really?

I wasn't a utility. By this stage I was a specialist half. I couldn't play in the middle and truck it up as a forward. I couldn't catch bombs at fullback or the wing. And I couldn't run crash lines on the edges. I couldn't make 40 tackles if I had to go on as a hooker.

But I wasn't about to say no.

'Yeah, sweet,' I said, fingers crossed. 'I'll play anywhere you put me.'

I arrived in camp to be surrounded by legends. Locky was there, of course. Petero Civoniceva, too. And then there was Andrew Johns.

We got straight into training and I was thrown in both No. 7 and No. 6. I went into the halves to fill in for both Locky and Joey during the training drills. And I was blown away. The skill level on display was out of this world. I thought the Queensland sessions were as good as it got. I was wrong.

Watching the speed, accuracy and skill of these players was inspiring. Seeing the ball go from Danny Buderus (Bedsy), to Joey, to Locky was a sight I will never forget. Everything at that session was just on the money. Next level.

I remember taking a mental note: *This is how it's done. This is how I have to do it. This is how good you need to be.*

It only reinforced my view that I was a long way off being anywhere near as complete as Andrew Johns.

The match was played in front of almost 45,000 people at Lang Park. I sat on the bench for most of the first half, finally getting the call when fullback Karmichael Hunt was taken from the field after being knocked out. Ricky shifted Locky to No. 1 and put me on at No. 6 to partner Joey in the halves.

I had to pinch myself. I had fulfilled my dream of playing with Locky but I never thought I would get the chance to play with Joey. My rival was now my teammate. It had been almost a year since Joey destroyed me during State of Origin. Now I was going to get to do the destroying with him.

And it was extraordinary. I only called the ball a few times, but he hit me on the chest with a bullet on every occasion. I was a bit timid but he made it easy. He was awesome.

We ended up winning the Anzac test 50–12, but it wasn't as easy as the score might suggest. It was a physical game and I got bashed. No matter what the score is, when you play the Kiwis, you know you have been in a game. They are intense and don't stop hitting. They run hard and tackle hard.

Joey retired suddenly in 2007 when he was struck down by a career-ending neck injury. It was a strange feeling to know I would never play against him again. It was a sad day for rugby league.

I ended up having the privilege of playing against him on five occasions in the NRL. I won that battle 3–2. He got me 2–0 when it came to Origin. Of course, my best memory of Joey is playing alongside him in that Test match. That is when I really saw his genius.

The rest of the NRL season was very forgettable as far as I am concerned. We would only win another five matches that year. Yes: five. After starting the year with six straight wins we went on to lose 13 matches to finish in ninth place and miss the finals by two points.

CHAPTER THIRTY

QUEENSLAND WERE UNDER THE pump coming into the 2006 State of Origin series. We were facing humiliation. We were on the verge of becoming the first Queensland team to lose four State of Origin series in a row. We would be the biggest embarrassment in Maroons history if we couldn't find a way to beat New South Wales.

Few rugby league followers gave us hope, but we felt New South Wales were vulnerable, especially in the halves. But again we lost Game I.

We were left reeling. Everyone in Queensland was filthy. Everyone in New South Wales was laughing at us. The media were saying we might even kill Origin. Apparently people were losing interest because it was all so one-sided.

The papers were brutal, going after our leadership group. They were demanding the heads of our senior players: Lockyer, Price and Petero Civoniceva. They were saying it was their fault and they should be sacked. These guys were Queensland legends. Heart-and-soul players.

And boy, did the sacking calls fire us up.

Under the pump, knives in our backs, sides and fronts, in Game II we came out and belted the Blues 30–6 in a record State of Origin flogging. And we did it amid a shocking injury toll that forced us to play with a side that everyone had claimed would be embarrassed.

Still no one gave us a chance of winning Game III. Of stopping the Blues from creating history by becoming the first side to win four in a row. And the press turned up the heat by calling for our captain's head.

In a completely unfair attack, they said Locky was too old. They said he was too slow and that he could no longer defend.

'I want to say a few words,' Lockyer said on the night before the match, to be played at the Telstra Dome in Melbourne. 'We've copped a hammering. No one gives us a hope. Most of it has been about me and I apologise for that. I can see that it's been affecting you. I can't do anything about what's been said, but I can do something about what will happen on the field tomorrow night.

'I'm going to go out there and be the best player on the field. I'm going to win you guys this match. And I want every one of you to go in thinking the same way as I am. Think that you'll be the best on the field. Think that it will be you that wins us the game. If we all do that then we can't lose.'

We ran out knowing it was do-or-die for our captain and for the dignity of our state.

Locky's message was ringing in my ear. *Be the best player on the field. Win the match for your side.*

The game started well, with Mogg continuing his try-scoring form to land the first four-pointer of the night.

Then I stuffed up.

Going for the throat in the 25th minute, out to bury the Blues, I threw a Hail Mary pass to Adam Mogg in an attempt to send him over for his second. I saw that he was unmarked, but I didn't see Eric Grothe flying through.

No. No. No.

I turned and chased, cursing myself as I ran. Eric Grothe was sprinting down the line after plucking the miscued pass from the air. There was no catching the NSW winger, who ran almost 100 metres to score.

You won't see that on my Origin highlights reel.

Locked at 4–all at the break, New South Wales stole the lead in the 46th minute when Matt King touched down to make it 10–4 following the conversion. And then came the controversy – Grothe going in again to score after Brett Hodgson knocked the ball on. The decision was sent up to the video referee and we were certain the try would not be awarded. The ball, sent into the air by Craig Gower, had bounced forward off Hodgson's chest and then arm before Steve Menzies pounced to scoop it up to send Grothe over.

I was standing right next to the fullback when he dropped it. I even pulled my hands out of the way to make sure that I didn't make it a double knock-on.

TRY!

We were shocked when the decision came through, the green light flashing on the big screen. New South Wales celebrated like they had already won the game.

Locky pulled us all in. 'We can still do this,' he shouted. 'We are Queensland. Remember what the men who came before you have done in this jersey. We'll do it too.'

We were down 14–4 when we went about making a miracle.

In the 71st minute, clock ticking, Blues on the verge of the record-creating win, Clinton Schifcofske threw me the ball. He had been swung in the tackle and instinctively chucked it out the back. I was on my own 10-metre line when I caught it. I looked up and saw a bit of space, so I took it. I stepped back off my right foot and went through the line. I darted 20 metres before I saw Brent Tate (Tatey) on my outside. I threw the ball right and it stuck. He ran 60 metres to score under the posts.

We had seven minutes to save our state – we only needed one minute. In a moment of madness from Brett Hodgson, the fullback went into dummy half and threw a long ball. He missed his mark, the ball bouncing on the ground. And the man who made the pre-game promise to win us the game delivered on his word. Locky charged through and pounced on the ball before running 15 metres to score.

We held on for the last five minutes to win 16–14.

It was the greatest feeling of my life. Pure elation. Electric.

It was a whole new level from the 2004 grand final win.

And the celebration was huge.

What came next was a State of Origin dynasty.

CHAPTER THIRTY-ONE

IT TOOK JUST FOUR HOURS to sell out Suncorp Stadium for our triumphant State of Origin return to Queensland. The first 10,000 tickets were snapped up in just seven minutes, the rest all gone a few hours later.

A huge crowd, 52,498 screaming fans, mostly Queenslanders, were at the ground formerly known as Lang Park to give us a heroes' welcome as we ran out on the field to face the Blues in the first match of the 2007 State of Origin series. They would all become witnesses to rugby league history.

Soon we would become the first Maroons side since 1995 to win three consecutive State of Origin matches. Later we would become the only side in history to win eight series straight. Rugby league's most famous empire was being forged, the greatest dynasty in the game born.

After that match we felt invincible. It would never matter what was on the scoreboard: no matter how many points we were down, we always thought we would win. That comeback in Queensland gave us the belief, confidence and shot in the arm that would see us go on to win a record-making eight series in a row.

We won that record-making series in 2013, when we held on to beat the Blues at ANZ Stadium in a heart-stopping decider. As we went into the match locked on a win each, most commentators were saying New South Wales were 80 minutes away from ending our streak. They said the NSW home crowd would be enough to get them home.

It almost was.

After jumping out to a 12–4 lead in the 61st minute when Justin Hodges scored, the Blues mounted a comeback. The gap was slashed to just two points when Trent Merrin scored under the posts in the 70th minute and James Maloney kicked the conversion. The game would go down to the wire.

I thought we had scored the match-winning try soon after – but we were denied because of interference from a streaker called Wati. Yep. A big fella had ripped his gear off and run the length of the field in the nude before being hammered by security guards. He was tackled in front of me as I was passing to Ashley Harrison, who laid on what should have been the match-winner.

New South Wales got a final shot but we held on to seal the historic win. We had done it: eight in a row. It was a remarkable achievement. Unbelievable. We had gone from being the team that could have lost four in a row to the team that won eight in a row. And it was never easy.

People don't realise how close a lot of those games were. They don't remember the come-from-behind wins or the adversities we faced. New South Wales never went away. They were always a great side and always a chance to beat us. There were games where the Blues were the better team for most of the match. Games they should have won. There was never an easy match. All tough. All brutal.

It was big plays and our never-say-die attitude that got us home. It was errors and lapses that cost them.

I can't see another team repeating what we did. I don't think it will happen again.

* * *

Let's back it up a bit, rewind to 2008. The Rugby League World Cup, being held in Australia and New Zealand, is in full swing. I'm sitting on the Kangaroos team bus, clad in the green and gold of Australia, my training singlet sweat-soaked and covered in dirt.

Darren Lockyer is sitting behind me, Greg Inglis in front. I look around and see my mate Smithy; head resting against the glass, deep in contemplation. Behind him Petero Civoniceva is chatting to Israel Folau, the odd couple having a laugh.

I'm riding with rugby league royalty. And now, two years after making my debut for the Kangaroos, I feel like I belong. I'm no longer a rookie and I've earned my spot.

We have just finished training. The bus is rattling back towards our team hotel. We are well prepared to play Fiji in the semi-final of the World Cup in a couple of days in Sydney. We are one win away from competing for international rugby league's greatest prize. And after we kicked off our campaign with a 30–6 win over New Zealand at the Sydney Football

Stadium before flogging England 52–4 at Telstra Dome in Melbourne, I am sure the World Cup will be ours. I am on top of the world.

'Hey, Sam,' I say as I answer the call from my girlfriend.

'How are you?' she asks. 'What are you doing?'

I know something isn't quite right. Her voice ...

'What is it?' I ask. 'Don't worry about me. Is something wrong? Has something happened?'

And then my world, all perfect – World Cup wins and rugby league royalty – comes crashing down.

'It's your uncle,' Samantha says. 'It's Uncle Richard. He's been bashed. He's dead. He was murdered.'

I'm not sure how I responded to Sam. I'm not sure that I responded at all. Soon I was squeezing my mobile phone, call over and bus bouncing down the road. I stared out the window. Silent. Still. But soon I sobbed. I did my best not to cry, wary of making a scene in front of the boys, but the tears came.

'What is it, mate?' Locky asked, my childhood hero turned mate putting his arm around me after moving up a seat. 'What's happened?'

I told him my uncle had been murdered. Bashed to death. He gave me a hug and I cried some more. We stayed in that embrace for the rest of the ride.

'Let's go and see Ricky, mate,' he said when we arrived back at the hotel.

I shook my head. 'No,' I said. 'I'll keep it to myself.'

I didn't want to be a distraction. I didn't want to ruin our World Cup campaign.

'Na, mate,' Locky said. 'Put yourself first. We'll be right.'

Locky ended up convincing me that the team wouldn't suffer and that Sticky would help. He was right on both fronts. Ricky gave me both comfort and support. He told me that I had to put myself first and the team second. He told me I could leave camp and travel back to Brisbane to be with my family.

'No,' I said. 'I want to play. That's what my uncle would have wanted. I'll play this game for him and for my family.'

I knew the best thing for both me and them was to play that weekend. I had good support around me in the coaching staff and the playing group. I wanted to play the match for my family. I wanted to dedicate the game to my uncle. I wanted to give my family a bright moment to light up a very dark time.

'OK,' Ricky said. 'Are you sure?' I thought I was.

I tried to put it all out of my mind so I could focus on the game. But all alone in my hotel room, I couldn't stop thinking about my uncle. About what had happened to him.

I called a good mate who lived in Sydney. 'You free?' I asked. 'Want to hang out?'

We met up an hour or so later. I didn't tell him what had happened. I didn't want to talk about it. I didn't even want to think about it. But by the time he dropped me back to the hotel it was all over the news. I quickly learned the full details of what had happened.

Eight men had beaten my uncle, Richard Saunders, to death in Ewing Park, Woodridge, a suburb of Logan City in Brisbane.

My uncle had been drinking with some mates when an argument broke out with a group of teenagers who were passing through the park. The teenagers left – only to come back with another four men 10 minutes later. They bashed my uncle with a hammer, a fence paling, their fists and their feet. He was dead when they left.

Eight men, aged 16 to 26, were arrested.

It was horrific and confronting. I knew the area he lived in had some problems. He was from a tough neighbourhood where a lot of people were struggling to make ends meet. But I had no idea that anyone from that neighbourhood was capable of such violence. Of murder.

I was stunned.

My whole attitude to violence and community changed after that shocking moment. I think I realised that a lot of people were really struggling out there and that they needed help.

I work in disadvantaged communities as often as I can. I don't want to see another family left without a husband, a father, a brother, a son ... an uncle, because of a senseless act of violence.

Of course I can't stop things like this from happening, but I hope I can help ease a bit of community tension and stress, which contributed to my uncle's death.

I dedicated my next game, the match against Fiji, to my family. To my uncle. And I played one of my best games for the Kangaroos. I scored three tries and kicked six goals for a personal haul of 24 points in our 52–0 win over Fiji. I was awarded man of the match.

That award, a gold medal, now sits alongside my first Dally M. It means as much to me as any trophy I have ever won.

CHAPTER THIRTY-TWO

ANOTHER STANDOUT MATCH IN the green and gold of Australia came in 2012 when I replaced Darren Lockyer as the Kangaroos No. 6. The game was played in Eden Park, New Zealand, in the Anzac Test match on 20 April. There are only a couple of games where I can remember being nervous before a match – this was one of them.

I felt a ton of pressure before this game because I was going to wear a jersey that had belonged not only to a legend but also to one of my heroes. I guess I felt I had to do it justice.

Playing five-eighth for Australia was a big job in itself. But to do it after Lockyer? Yep, I felt like the weight of the world was on my shoulders – again. I guess it was a similar feeling to when I was being compared to Andrew

Johns a few years earlier. And just as before that game against the Knights, I was overwhelmed. I didn't sleep heading into the match. I tossed and turned, thinking of failure instead of success.

Don't embarrass Locky. Don't embarrass yourself.

I was lucky that I was comfortable playing alongside my teammates. Cooper Cronk came in to partner me in the halves. I had played plenty of footy with Coops by this time, so he made my transition to No. 6 easier than it could have been.

Smithy was also there of course, at No. 9 – steering the ship. Smithy replaced Darren Lockyer as the captain of Australia, and it was a seamless transition. He was the obvious choice, having already captained the Queensland Origin team. Smithy was just like Locky in that you thought you would never lose when he was in your team. He gave us all confidence that we would prevail, no matter what.

I never got to captain Australia – or Queensland – and that might have bothered me had it not been for Cameron Smith. He was always the best person for the job. Anyway, I wasn't thinking about the captaincy before the Eden Park match.

I went on to play one of my best matches for Australia, putting in a man-of-the-match performance in a comfortable win. I was in my element as soon as I took to the field. I scored a try and ended up forgetting all about the pressure.

The trainer, being directed by the coach, actually tried to get me to come off towards the end of the game. Daly Cherry-Evans was on the bench and they wanted to bring him on.

'No!' I screamed. 'No way.'

I was going to finish the game. I told them they would have to drag me off. I had put myself through the wringer that week and there was no way I was going to give up that jersey now that I had it. It has always been in the back of my mind that any game could be my last for Australia; an injury could end my career or for whatever ever reason I might not be selected again.

I wanted every minute I could get. That is an attitude I kept to the end. I always fought with the trainers when they asked me to come off, and I always asked to play when the coach offered to rest me for a game.

Anyway, I got my way and they left me on. I walked off the field – after 80 minutes – happy with both the team's performance and my own. I didn't think I was any Darren Lockyer, but I certainly hadn't embarrassed myself or him.

The following year I took part in the 2013 World Cup tour in the UK. We had plenty of fun on the football field. We were untouchable; we only conceded 22 points during the entire tour.

It was an old-school style of tour where we had plenty of good times and played plenty of good football. The side itself was awesome. We had superstars like Smithy, Inglis, Darius Boyd, Cronk and Matt Scott all playing in their prime. Jarryd Hayne and Brett Morris both scored four tries each in our 62–0 quarter final win over the USA.

The World Cup final, played at Old Trafford, wasn't even close – the Kiwis were never in it. We belted them 34–2 in one of the most lopsided matches I can remember against New Zealand.

The whole week I could tell we would win. Our preparation was perfect and everyone in the team was oozing confidence. I was personally in my prime. I got the man-of-the-match award in the four games that I played.

Manchester United, arguably the greatest soccer club in the world, invited me, Smithy and Paul Gallen (Gal) to tour their ground and training facility – Old Trafford in Manchester – during the tour.

English legends Rio Ferdinand, Michael Carrick and Ryan Giggs were waiting for us when we arrived.

'How good is this?' Smithy said. 'You know how famous these blokes are?'

I nodded.

They were three of the biggest names in world sport.

'Yeah, they ain't going to know us,' I said. 'Who are we in England?'

Now Smithy was nodding.

'JT,' Giggs said, rushing forward to shake my hand. 'How good was that try you scored in State of Origin?'

I was stunned. *Really? You saw that?*

Turns out Manchester United had attended the 2013 State of Origin decider at ANZ Stadium earlier that year, when I scored under the posts in our 12–10 win.

'Yeah, I liked that try,' Giggs said. I went red, completely chuffed.

We exchanged jerseys and had a chat before he led us on a tour of the famous facility. And wow! What a facility it was. They had recovery centres, gyms and cinema rooms. Spas, saunas and chefs. They even had a bloke washing the players' cars – Bentleys, Ferraris and Lamborghinis – in the car park.

'Reckon I could get someone to Dairy Farmers Stadium to wash my Toyota?' I said to Smithy.

We were soon looking at their practice pitch. 'Really,' I said. 'A training field.'

The ground was perfect, the greenest grass I had ever seen. And the field was surrounded by stands that were bigger than we have at some NRL grounds. 'What about all the other fields?' I asked, pointing to the other playing pitches. There were at least another 10.

'Oh, they're for all the junior teams,' Giggs said. 'The one furthest away is for the Under 8s academy team. The closest is for our second team.'

Giggs pointed. 'I think Beckham is over there somewhere watching his son train,' he said.

David Beckham was one of the biggest stars in the world in 2013. He was a household name across the globe.

'You're geeing me up, right?' I asked. Turns out he wasn't.

Smithy shouted. 'Is that David Beckham?'

'No way,' I replied. I looked out the window of the bus, our tour of Old Trafford over. 'Is it?' I said as I jumped up. 'It is. Stop the bus.' I bolted down the aisle before hurtling out the door. 'Becks!' I screamed and I sprinted. 'BECKS!'

He was about 100 metres away and I was closing fast. 'Becks!' I shouted again.

He stopped and turned. He looked terrified, seeing a crazy fella rushing towards him. I realised he thought I was a lunatic. I didn't care.

'Sir,' I said, being unable to think of anything better to say. 'Sir. SIR. S.I.R.'

He stopped and waited.

'Sir,' I said again, puffing and panting when I finally reached him. 'I'm sorry but I just had to meet you. I'm on a tour with the Australian rugby league team and I saw you.'

He nodded.

'I understand if you say no, but is there any chance I can get a picture with you?'

He nodded again. 'Yeah, of course,' Beckham said.

It was then I realised I had no one to take the photo. It was going to have to be my first ever selfie.

‘JT,’ Smithy said, appearing from nowhere. ‘I’ll take it.’

Smithy and Gal had chased down Beckham too. We were all starstruck, mouths open, legs shaking. Beckham had no idea who we were but he stood around chatting with us all the same. He was a bloody legend and it was some moment. He was a rockstar, all cool and looking mint. We eventually made it back to the bus. I was stoked.

CHAPTER THIRTY-THREE

DR CHRIS SARRA SAT us down in a room in the lead-up to the first ever NRL All Stars clash in 2010. The famous Indigenous rights and education campaigner had been brought in to talk to the Indigenous All Stars team about what it meant to be Aboriginal.

'So who are you?' Dr Sarra asked. 'And where do you come from?'

I shrugged. I wasn't alone.

'No, really,' he continued. 'What do you know about your family? About your past? Who are your ancestors? What did they do and how did they help you become the person you are today?'

Again I shrugged, giving him a blank look.

'Go and stand on that side of the room if you can

answer those questions,' he continued. 'Stay where you are if you can't.'

I stood completely still.

All I knew was that I considered myself to be Aboriginal. I didn't know about my family or their history. I didn't know how my ancestors helped me become the person who was standing in that room on that day. And I was a little bit embarrassed. I had been selected to play in the Indigenous All Stars team that would take on the NRL All Stars and I knew little of what it meant to be Indigenous.

'Mum, I need to know more about our family,' I said to my mother after I returned home from the match.

I had just won the first ever Preston Campbell Medal for man of the match during our 16–12 win over the NRL All Stars on the Gold Coast.

'Can you tell me about our family? About our history?'

Mum smiled. 'I'll do better than that,' she replied. 'You can go see it yourself.'

So Mum organised for me to travel back to where she grew up. She gave my Uncle Mark a call and asked him to take me out to Mitchell in the Western Downs district of the Maranoa Region, Queensland.

Uncle Mark was the most knowledgeable when it came to my family history and culture. He was more than happy to take me back to Mitchell and introduce me to all my relatives who still lived there.

We hired a minivan, uncles and cousins piling in, and made the six-hour trip from Brisbane.

Mitchell is a sheep and cattle town with a population of just over 1000. I spent the weekend there, staying with family I had never met. I had cousins, aunties and uncles everywhere. Uncle Mark showed us the old watering holes that he and my mum used to swim in as kids and the fields where they would play. I saw their school and the house where they were raised. I remember having a conversation with my mother when I got back. 'I feel like I've been there before,' I said. 'It all seemed so familiar. I was relaxed as soon as I got there. At peace.'

And I was. I had a real connection with Mitchell and it was quite an emotional experience going there. I found out a lot of my history and I felt a better connection with my past.

Mostly I remember little stories about my family. Not struggles or life-changing stuff, but tidbits that told me a bit about who they were. Like the story about my pop and how he got the nickname 'Finnegan'. Apparently Pop was always following an Irish bloke called Finnegan around, because he played a musical instrument. Pop loved music and was always around him trying to learn how to play. So they started calling him Finnegan. I like that story because it told me a little bit about who my pop was.

I came back from the trip a different person. After hearing stories about my family I decided I needed to make some stories of my own. I knew I had to do more with my life in terms of making a difference. I wanted to make sure I did all I could to be remembered for the right reasons.

Apart from my visit to Mitchell, I remember 2010 for being all about contracts and cash. For being a circus. I was to be a free agent the following year and I was getting offers from everywhere.

I have to say the money being offered, especially from French and Japanese rugby clubs, was tempting. But my girlfriend, Samantha, told me my career was more important than cash.

'You haven't done your job here, Johnathan,' she said. 'You won't be remembered as a legend of the game if you leave the NRL now. You'll never be an immortal. You'll be forgotten. And you haven't won that premiership you've always said you have to win for the Cowboys.'

She was right. I loved Townsville. I loved the Cowboys. And I had an unquenched thirst to bring North Queensland their first ever title. The thought of leaving the Cowboys, walking out without winning a premiership, was too much to contemplate.

I was stoked when the Cowboys signed Coops for 2011. And I was a kid in a candy shop when he finally turned up in Townsville. Gavin Cooper is my biggest partner in rugby league crime and one of my best mates. I met Coops in 2005 when we were both recruited by the Cowboys. He was one of my first friends in Townsville and we stayed close even when he left to join the Titans at the end of 2006.

'Yeah, bra,' he said when we were reunited as Cowboys. 'Let's go and win you that premiership you're always talkin' about.'

I nodded.

Little did I know that he would help deliver me my dream just a few short years later – or that we would form one of the most potent partnerships in the NRL.

Coops returned to the Cowboys as a right-edge back- rower. I was on the left. It was only when Scott Bolton was injured that we were put together on the football field. We immediately clicked and went on to form an on-field partnership that would endure and thrive right up until my very last game. I would put him over for 29 tries over the next eight years. Our friendship will last forever.

Coops knows me better than anyone, both on and off the football field. He can see when I am struggling with something and he knows what to say to pick me up. He is also one of the only people who can read my body language on the football field.

'Pick ya lip up,' he says when he senses that I am frustrated. 'Get on with it.'

The 2011 season ended up being a much better year for us, both on and off the field. We won 14 games to storm into the finals for the first time since 2007. Unfortunately, we got pumped in our sudden-death semi, losing to Manly 42–8. I wasn't happy with the finals defeat, but there were certainly positive signs after four tough years.

CHAPTER THIRTY-FOUR

AFTER ANOTHER ROUND OF contract negotiations, 2012 was another year of improvement for the Cowboys as a team. Beating the Broncos 33–16 in the preliminary final – and watching on as a young bloke named Michael Morgan scored a hat-trick – was a season highlight. But we ultimately crashed out in the second week of the finals, losing to Manly in a 22–12 defeat.

On the field I knew I had to deliver. I knew I would be crucified if I didn't perform. Part of being a marquee signing is becoming an ambassador, a spokesman and a role model for the club. You have to work for sponsors, become a media go-to man, and play a leading role for the club in the community. In short, you have to work for every cent you're earning.

A lot of players struggle with money when they suddenly sign a big deal. We have all heard the horror stories of players left with nothing. Thankfully my manager has always looked after me when it comes to my money. Sammy put me in front of a financial advisor way back when I was at the Bulldogs, even though I was earning next to nothing. And he put me on a weekly allowance as soon as I moved to North Queensland. The rest of my money was put into building a property portfolio.

I could easily be in a sad situation now had it not been for the good people around me.

I was hoping to concentrate on football once I signed the four-year deal that would almost make me a Cowboy for life – but 2013 was going to be another difficult year.

We spent most of the season dealing with speculation surrounding the future of our coach, Neil Henry. The press labelled him a dead man walking after we crashed to our ninth loss of the year in round 13 – and by July he was indeed told his contract would not be renewed.

We made the finals in 2013, finishing eighth, but we were knocked out by Cronulla 20–18 in the first week of the finals.

The year finished well for me personally with the Rugby League International Federation (RLIF) presenting me with my second Golden Boot for best player in the world.

I didn't know a lot about Paul Green until he arrived as our new coach. A former Cowboys player, he had coached Wynnum Manly to consecutive premierships in the Intrust Super Cup before joining Trent Robinson as an assistant at the Roosters.

Greeny changed so much in such a short time. He came to Townsville and put a broom through the club.

'You can't win away from home,' he said during an honesty session, conducted on a pre-season camp on the Gold Coast. 'You can't win without JT. You have a soft underbelly. You are not a serious footy team. That is how everyone on the outside perceives this club.'

Greeny asked us what we would like to be known for. How we would like people outside the club to think of us. We came up with our answers and they became our goals and mission statement. I won't reveal what they were because they are still used by the club today.

Personally I knew Greeny would get the best out of me. He pulled me aside early on and gave me permission to play anywhere I saw fit on the football field. Previously I had been locked on an edge. I could now play on both sides of the ruck. Greeny brought to the club a training style that I had never seen before. It appeared casual, but the intensity that was required when he meant business was next-level. He trained smarter – not necessarily harder. He had a big emphasis on skill – it was at a higher intensity than we had ever done before.

From the day he arrived, I knew we would win a premiership under him. It didn't happen in 2014 but 2015 was a different story.

Our season looked like going from bad to worse. We had lost our first three games but a back-from-the-dead win against the Storm kick-started our run. We went on to win our next 11 games and record the biggest winning streak in the club's history.

Nothing could stop us.

We got behind in a lot of those games but we always found a way out. We had that belief that we could win no matter what. We didn't look at the clock. We didn't look at the score. We mounted our biggest ever comeback to beat the Eels 36–30 in round 13, and we beat the Raiders with a field goal on the buzzer in a round 15 classic. None of those games were easy – but we just did whatever it took to win.

I knew it was our year.

We were in that magical place they call the 'zone'. All the boys were at another level that year. Michael Morgan (Morgo), Lachlan Coote (Cootey), Jake Granville (Jakey), Jason Taumalolo (Jase), Gavin Cooper (Coops), Matt Scott (Thumper), James Tamou, Kyle Feldt (Feldty), Justin O'Neill (Juzzy) – they were all at their best.

I was at the peak of my powers. I ended up winning my fourth Dally M by 11 points. I had some great years – winning the Golden Boot in 2011 and 2013, and the Dally M in 2005, 2007 and 2014 – but 2015 was my most complete.

In 2015 I excelled both at club level and on the representative stage. I became the only player in history to win four Dally Ms, and my life changed to the extent that I couldn't go out in public without being mobbed. It became ridiculous. I couldn't work it out. I already had three Dally Ms but for some reason that fourth made me super-famous. I wouldn't say I struggled with it, but the intensity of public scrutiny just took off.

And that went up again after the premiership. We, of course, combined to deliver North Queensland the title when we beat the Broncos 17–16 in my golden point field goal fairytale.

I was awarded the Golden Boot at the end of 2015 to cap off the best year of my life.

Kicking a field goal in extra time to deliver North Queensland their first ever title was the defining moment of my career. It was my legacy. I was brought to the Cowboys in 2005 to win the club a premiership and I got to be a part of that in 2015.

It was the best moment of my career and a part of rugby league history that can never be erased. I am happy for that game and the match-winning moment to define my career. And not just for me or because of me, more because of what it meant for my club, my teammates, my coaching staff and most importantly the Cowboys fans.

CHAPTER THIRTY-FIVE

I WENT INTO THE 2014 State of Origin series expecting our record-making run of eight to become nine. With only one change to the team that did the job in 2013 – Aidan Guerra coming in for the injured Sam Thaiday – and two of the three matches to be played in Queensland, I was sure we would win. The dynasty would continue.

But it didn't.

New South Wales came out swinging in the opener and beat us 12–8 in a Suncorp Stadium shock. After Darius Boyd went over in the corner to score the first try, the Blues went in twice – first Brett Morris and then Jarryd Hayne – to leave us trailing 10–4 at half-time.

Trent Hodkinson kicked a penalty goal in the 42nd minute to extend New South Wales' lead to 8 – and that would be enough for the Blues to win.

We mounted a comeback, of course, Boyd scoring again in the 56th minute to make it 12–8. We went close in the 74th – but Brett Morris denied Boyd his third. We went close in the 78th – but Hayne denied Chris McQueen. And we went close in the 79th – but Daly Cherry-Evans was stopped three metres short. We lost.

I didn't see the defeat coming. I didn't think we were vulnerable heading into the series. I didn't think the Blues had a better team.

We went to Sydney on a mission to save the series – we failed, the record-breaking run over after a gut-wrenching two-point loss.

In a 6–4 win to New South Wales that was hailed in the press as the beginning of a Blues era, New South Wales defeated us to win their first State of Origin series in nine years.

I didn't like losing too much. It was a bad feeling. Only three or four of us in the team had ever lost a series before. It was new and shattering for everyone else. It was certainly hard to take after what we had done the year before.

But full credit to New South Wales – they won by executing their big plays. That proved the difference.

The difference between winning and losing in Origin is taking your chances.

We came together, a tight huddle, and spoke about not wanting to feel the heartbreak of a series loss again. We vowed to make up for it, both in Game III and then the following year. The media was claiming the dynasty was over, that the Blues would now go on a record-breaking run.

But while our unbroken streak of eight was officially over, we were far from a fading force. We proved as much when we blitzed the Blues 32–8 in Game III, before going on to reclaim the series in 2015. We won Game I by a single point before New South Wales forced it to a third match by beating us in Game II. We then went on to demolish the Blues with a record-breaking 52–6 romp in the decider. I kicked a record-making nine goals from nine attempts.

That game was the only Origin match I can say was easy. It was the only Origin game where I always felt in control. That was some freakish performance. It was also the end of an era.

* * *

After a tough run with injuries, a shoulder operation and months of rehabilitation, I was ready to begin my final season in the NRL. I wanted to run a victory lap with my mates. I wanted to hoist the Provan-Summons Trophy into the night air. I wanted to find my wife in the sea of blue, yellow and white at ANZ Stadium – and kiss her before hugging my girls, Frankie, Charlie and Lillie.

I wanted to end my career with a premiership but it ended up being one of the most difficult years in my 17 NRL seasons.

I set the bar high when I began my final pre-season. Shoulder strong, body fresh, I thought I could turn back the clock and be at my best. I never once considered that my body would fail me.

I signed my final contract at the beginning of 2017 – a one-year deal – and I was adamant that I would be in my prime. I was comfortable with my decision both to play in 2018, and to retire at the end of that year. And I was planning on going out with a bang. I'd had a good look at the Cowboys NRL roster before agreeing to the deal.

'What a team,' I thought. 'Have a look at these names.' We had retained all our senior players, guys like

Matt Scott, Gavin Cooper, Coen Hess, Michael Morgan and Jason Taumalolo. We had also recruited Australian Test prop Jordan McLean.

I was confident we had a premiership-winning team when I signed the deal, and almost certain we could win the competition when I started my final pre-season. I looked at all the men on the training field and thought I was going to finish with a fairy tale.

We had basically the same team that had shocked rugby league by making the grand final in 2017. The only difference was that me and Matty Scott – two players with Test experience – would be back from injury. And as I said, Jordan McLean – the incumbent Kangaroos prop – had joined us fresh from his premiership win with the Storm. We were installed as pre-season favourites to win our second title.

Yep. Things were looking good.

The season started with a celebration: a round 1 win in my 300th game. With my family and friends in the stands, I celebrated my milestone with a 20–14 win over the Sharks.

I don't often think about records or numbers, but this one was very important to me. Not too many players get to 300 – in fact, only 31 players in the history of the game. Of all the things I have achieved in rugby league, this is the number that makes me really proud, because as a kid I would have been happy just to play one NRL match.

Too skinny. Too small. He'll never make it.

I thought of all the knockers and knock-backs when I played my 300th game. I thought of all the trials and tribulations. I thought of those tracksuits I was never given and sweeping the floor in the butcher's shop.

Wow. 300? Who would have thought?

Terry Lamb, Steve Menzies, Cliff Lyons, Andrew Ettingshausen, Paul Langmack ... suddenly my name was alongside some of the toughest and most enduring players to have ever strapped on a boot. Any player who makes the NRL is good. Well, not just good, but outstanding. And of those who do end up making it into the top grade, the average length of a career in the NRL is just 43 games. So to make the 300 club was both an honour and a privilege.

I celebrated with family and friends after the game before making a vow to get on with the year. I wasn't going to think about milestones or the fact it was my final season – my focus was to be solely on the Cowboys, and leading them to a premiership. I didn't want to be distracted – or to be a distraction – from leading North Queensland to NRL wins.

At least that was the plan.

CHAPTER THIRTY-SIX

WE LOST OUR NEXT five games – beginning with a 24–20 heartbreaker to the Broncos – to put a huge dent in our premiership credentials. Our 27–10 loss to the Bulldogs at home in round 6 was particularly hard to take, given my old club were struggling and tipped for a tough year.

The rugby league critics were beginning to doubt we were the real deal, and the losses had certainly put us on the back foot. Injuries to Jordan McLean, Javid Bowen and Kane Linnett were also a cause for concern.

I left no stone unturned trying to help my team break out of our slump. I wasn't happy with my form, and I trained as hard as I could and remained positive in a bid to lift the team.

Our second win of the year came in round 7, when we beat the Titans 26–14 at home. We made it three in round 9 by beating the Panthers by six in Bathurst. But then we dropped back-to-back games to all but end our season.

A heartbreaking one-point loss to Souths at home in round 11 meant that we would need a miracle to make the finals. Still I hadn't given up hope, but I knew we would probably be playing the rest of the season for pride.

My year went from bad to worse when Queensland lost the State of Origin series to New South Wales. After going down to the Blues 22–12 at the MCG in Game I, the Maroons surrendered the shield for just the second time in 13 years when they lost to New South Wales by four points at ANZ Stadium in Game II.

I found watching the second game, from the Channel 9 box where I was working as a guest commentator, particularly difficult, because I thought it was a game we should have won.

I hadn't been out in public – unless absolutely necessary – since the celebrations that followed my 300th game.

The year had begun with the promise of a fairy tale premiership finish and by round 19 we were fighting to avoid the wooden spoon. I really struggled to deal with both my form and the form of the team. I took every loss personally and refused to believe we were out of the premiership hunt until it became a mathematical impossibility.

I would go so far as to say it was the most challenging season of my football career. We had a team that was capable of winning the competition. I was fit and should have been firing. But for whatever reason the team couldn't put it together – and neither could I.

I trained as hard as I could and did everything I could to turn it around – but it wasn't to be. Nothing worked. We kept on losing.

I was at training, kicking stones, when one of the boys cracked a joked. I have no idea what it was, but it made me laugh.

Ha! Ha! Ha!

It was then I realised what it was I would miss most about rugby league. I wouldn't wake up in 2019 missing the premiership rings, the Dally Ms or the last-minute wins. I would miss my mates.

I was struggling not only with my form and the prospect of ruining my legacy, but also with my looming retirement. I was going to miss rugby league and I didn't know what I would do without football.

So enjoy it while you can.

I decided I would soak it all up. To stop worrying and start savouring. I was going to enjoy the rest of the year with my mates. I was going to laugh and high-five, and above all I was going to smile.

A sellout crowd of 25,095 turned out to 1300SMILES Stadium for my last ever game in North Queensland.

Wow!

I got tingles up and down my spine as I ran out, crowd roaring, flags waving, opposition team lining up to applaud me as I took the field.

And then I saw my mum. 'Go get 'em, son,' she said as she embraced me. 'Have a good game.'

The entire week leading into the game had been overwhelming – tributes, fanfare and text messages from family and friends – and now I was hugging my mum on the edge of the field.

'Thanks, Mum,' I said, doing my best not to cry. 'Thanks for everything.'

I shook my head, trying to shake away the emotion.

I couldn't think of my friends and family, all in a private box the Cowboys had provided for the game, or the thousands of people in the stands holding JT signs and screaming my name. I had a football game to play.

And it ended up being some game. On a perfect night in Townsville, we destroyed the Eels 44–6. Ben Hampton opened the scoring in the fourth minute when he touched down for a try, and it didn't stop until the 53rd minute when I converted a try scored by Coops to bring us to 44. We were on fire. No one would have stopped us.

I had managed to hold back the tears before the match, but there was no controlling myself after the game. Not when my wife, Samantha, and my daughters Frankie and Charlie met me on the field with kisses and cuddles.

Not when the full house of Cowboys fans turned the flashes on their mobile phones into 25,000 shimmering stars in the chock-a-block stands.

And definitely not when Gavin Cooper and Matt Scott launched me onto their shoulders and chaired me from the ground like a king.

EPILOGUE

IN FEBRUARY 2018, I PROUDLY launched the Johnathan Thurston Academy. My hope is that the Academy will establish itself as a leading national provider of employment with training programs aimed at health, wellbeing, sport and education across Australia. I am really committed to supporting individuals to reach their personal, educational and career goals.

The thought of life without rugby league scares me. It is all I have ever known and the one thing I enjoy above all.

I still don't know who I will be without rugby league. I genuinely love the game. It has been a rollercoaster, with highs and lows, twists and turns, flat-out and a slow climb, and I didn't want to get off.

I will miss that two-minute bell. That moment when the game is about to start and you are looking into the eyes of your mates before telling them you are ready to give them all you have.

I will miss being a rugby league warrior. While the NRL will still be a big part of my life, I have fought my last battle. There will be no more wars. No more rivalries. No more teammates.

I am a gladiator gone.

I hope you have enjoyed the ride.

Always, JT.

JOHNATHAN THURSTON

THE CAREER

NRL

323 Games (29 Bulldogs, 294 Cowboys)

178 Wins (20 Bulldogs, 158 Cowboys)

90 Tries (10 Bulldogs, 80 Cowboys)

923 Goals (third-most all-time)

2222 Points (third-most all-time)

Premierships (Bulldogs 2004, Cowboys 2015)

The Deadlys Indigenous NRL Player of the Year Award (2006, 2007, 2009, 2011, 2013)

Preston Campbell Medal (2010, 2017)

RLPA Players' Champion Award (2005, 2013, 2014, 2015)

Arthur Beetson Medal (2017)

Provan-Summons Medal (2014, 2015)

Clive Churchill Medal (2015)

Dally M Medal (2005, 2007, 2014, 2015)

STATE OF ORIGIN

37 Games (24 wins, 5 tries)

99 Goals (most all-time)

220 Points (most all-time)

Wally Lewis Medal (2008)

Peter Jackson Memorial Trophy (2012, 2017)

WORLD CLUB CHALLENGE

Graham Murray Medal (2016)

TESTS

38 Games (35 wins, 13 tries)

165 Goals (most for Australia)

382 Points (most for Australia)

Harry Sunderland Medal (2013)

GOLDEN BOOT AWARD FOR BEST PLAYER IN THE WORLD

(2011, 2013, 2015)

HUMANITARIAN AWARDS

Ken Stephen Medal (2012)

Honorary Doctorate of Letters, James Cook University (2015)

Australian Human Rights Commission Medal (2017)

Queensland Australian of the Year (2018)

ACKNOWLEDGMENTS

IT'S TIME TO THANK some of the people who have played a role in making me both the player I was and the person I am.

I'll start with my mum and dad: Thanks for helping make my dream come true. None of this would have happened without your love, support, encouragement and unwavering belief. I hope I've made you proud.

To my brothers and sister, Robert, Shane, Katrina: I love you all. Thank you for always being there, for your support, your love and your loyalty.

To Uncle Dean: You are my guardian angel. I will be forever thankful to you for always looking after me.

To the rest of my uncles, aunties and cousins, we are forever family. You all played a part in shaping and developing me into the man I am today and for that I am eternally grateful. Your place in my childhood has given me some of my fondest memories. I may not see you often but you are always in my thoughts and forever in my heart.

To Uncle Richard: You are alive in my memory and in my heart.

To Nan and Chops: I think of you often and will love you always. I hope I've made you proud and that you're looking down on me with a smile on your face.

To Sam Ayoub: I might still be playing park football if it wasn't for you and whatever it was you saw in me. I cannot thank you enough for taking a chance with me, for your loyalty and dedication. It has been a hell of a ride and I couldn't think of anyone better to have shared it with.

To Peter Parr and Laurence Lancini: Thanks for convincing me to become a Cowboy. Words cannot do justice to how grateful I am to the both of you; for your loyalty, your advice, support and ultimately your friendship. You've both been there for me when no one else was and I hope in some small way, I've repaid you. You both give everything and expect nothing in return. I have the utmost love and respect for you and look forward to many more years of friendship.

I also have to thank my sponsors, in particular ASICS, Skins, Madison, the Toyota Motor Corporation and the North Queensland Toyota Dealers. Your belief and support allowed me to concentrate on becoming the best footballer I could be. I hope I've lived up to your expectations and look forward to continuing our long-standing relationships. Thanks again.

To Mal Meninga: Thank you for being a mentor and a mate. You weren't afraid to tell me what I needed to hear. You challenged me to be better in every way. Thanks for the lessons, sometimes hard, learned.

To Darren Lockyer, a hero who became a great mate. You're truly an inspiration and I consider myself so fortunate to have spent time with you on and off the field – you had a profound effect on my representative career, so thank you.

To Cameron Smith: Where do I start? My journey would have been nowhere near as enjoyable without you. The best thing about playing football is the mates you make and your friendship is most definitely a testament to that. You're a once-in-a-lifetime footballer and a once-in-a-lifetime friend. You've been a constant source of inspiration, motivation and confidence for me.

Samantha and I love your family dearly and look forward to holidays with you, Barb and the kids. Now let's get to that bucket list.

To Gavin Michael Cooper: My roomie! Thanks for the greatest times – both on and off the field. You know me inside out and back to front. You know exactly what to say and when to say it to pick me up and make me laugh. You were my partner in crime. We have shared the highs and lows and your friendship has been a constant in my life. I have so much love and respect for you and can't wait to continue our journey.

To Jamie Fitzpatrick: My confidant! Thanks for your guidance, friendship and loyalty. You've been there for me during the tough times and helped me make some of the biggest decisions in my life. Throughout it all, you've always had my best interests at heart. Who knows where I'd be today without you. Here's to the next chapter!

To all the clubs that honoured me with a farewell presentation, thank you. It was something I never expected and I was honestly humbled. They were moments I very much appreciated and will never forget.

To James Phelps, my publisher Helen Littleton and the team at HarperCollins Publishers Australia:

Thanks for all your work on this book. Phelpsy, you've been a mate for a long time and there could not have been a better writer for this book.

You don't get to where I am in my life without a lot of help from a lot of great people so I'd also like to make mention of: Paul Canning, Gary Reen, Mick Kennedy, Leo Reynolds, the Seddon family, Rob Walmsley and Kate Fahey, Steve Folkes, Ricky Stuart, Steve Price, Willie Tonga, Sam Thaiday, Billy Slater, Steve Walters, Kevin Walters, Allan Langer, Gaz Carden, Kevin Moore, Willie Mason, Graham Murray, Neil Henry, Paul Green, Steve Sartori, Dr Chris Ball, Matt Scott, Michael Morgan, Paul Bowman, Matthew Bowen, Paul Rauhihi, Matt Sing, Mark Fitzgerald, Phil Gould and Denis Handlin.

And most importantly to Sam, Frankie, Charlie, Lillie and Remie: You are the loves of my life. I will treasure you and love you until my final breath.

There are so many others who had a lasting impact on me personally and my career; to all of you … THANK YOU!

JOHNATHAN THURSTON ACADEMY

Inspiring individuals, encouraging education and overall wellbeing.

The JT Academy, established in 2018 with bases in Sydney and Brisbane, aims to be a leading national provider of outstanding employment initiatives and training programs aimed at health, wellbeing, sport and education across Australia. The academy's key strength is developing and delivering high-quality programs to individuals, equipping them with the right skills, knowledge and attributes to make a significant and positive future impact. Through strong education, community and industry partnerships we are committed to supporting people of all ages to reach their personal, educational and career goals.

JTLEARNING

Through online learning, the Johnathan Thurston Academy is powered by GO1, an online learning platform equipped to facilitate learning for users across a range of topics. Our content is targeted to support children, youth, adults and organisations across all industries to address the changing needs of individuals and organisations.

JTCOMMUNITY

Johnathan Thurston Academy develops and delivers a range of community programs and initiatives focusing on education, employment, health and wellbeing to assist our local communities. Through community consultation our programs are developed to support disadvantaged and marginalised youth and their families through delivery of capacity building programs. Our key programs include: JTBelieve (school engagement) JTWomenToLead (encouraging young women to think big and be bold) and JTSucceed (employment participation).

JTEMPLOYMENT

Johnathan Thurston Academy, with Lendlease as our major employment partner, is a unique collaborative employment zone. The goal and focus is to connect jobseekers to all of our employment partners including (but not limited to) Lendlease projects and communities throughout Queensland, New South Wales and the Northern Territory.

We aim to ensure that all opportunities for potential connections are both exhausted and managed in the one zone. We have created a unique and sophisticated platform that streamlines all employment and training opportunities between jobseekers and employers.

The main objective of the Academy is to ensure that locals throughout the regions have access to employment and training opportunities. We will link and connect with local community, government departments, schools, sub-contractors, retailers, project operations, local councils and all key community and industry stakeholders.

The JTJobBoard (jtacademy.com.au) is a hotspot for jobs across the nation, with some of Australia's biggest employers using the JTJobBoard to attract jobseekers and increase community workforce participation and engagement.

JTYOUTH

JTYouth zone provides a unique, safe place for young people to learn and engage with positive messaging. Sports, health, education, wellbeing and some creative activities. The JTYouth zone will welcome thousands of young people whom we will engage and provide positive messaging to raise their aspirations and provide them with access to high quality messaging, learning and activities.

For more information: www.jtacademy.com.au